Black Historical Figures

THE ARTS

TABLE OF CONTENTS

147 JUNE JORDAN

99 EDMONIA LEWIS

27 JAMES BALDWIN

These Workbooks are geared to intrigue, inspire and motivate you to want to learn more about these Black Historical Figures(BHFs) and others. Also to do more research on your own. We know this isn't all the history of these individuals. We want you to do some of the research also. We try to be as accurate as possible during our research. If there are some stories or questions that aren't as stated, please contact us at info@wegonnalearntoday.com.

Lorna Simpson

Lorna Simpson

August 13, 1960 – Present
PHOTOGRAPHER

3

Lorna Simpson

Lorna Simpson

Lorna Simpson

Lorna Simpson

Lorna Simpson

Hi, my name is Lorna Simpson. I was born on August 13, 1960, in Brooklyn, New York. I attended the High School of Art and Design in New York City and was an undergraduate at the New York School of Visual Arts. One of the things that I'm best known for is documentary photography. Some of the paintings that I'm known for are "You're Fine, You're Hired", "Corridor", "Three Figures" and "Unanswerable". I became the first African American woman in 1990 to exhibit at the Venice Biennale, which is an international arts festival. I've been the subject of solo shows at the Museum of Modern Art, the Brooklyn Museum and the Museum of Contemporary Art Chicago.

1. Where was I born?
   A. Chicago, IL
   B. Atlanta, GA
   C. Brooklyn, NY
2. I became the first African American woman to exhibit at?
   A. Manifesta
   B. Venice Biennale
   C. Whitney Biennial
3. Name a city where my art was featured at?
   A. Chicago
   B. Los Angeles
   C. Orlando

Directions: Answer the questions, to solve the crossword puzzle. You can use the internet if you get stuck on any question.

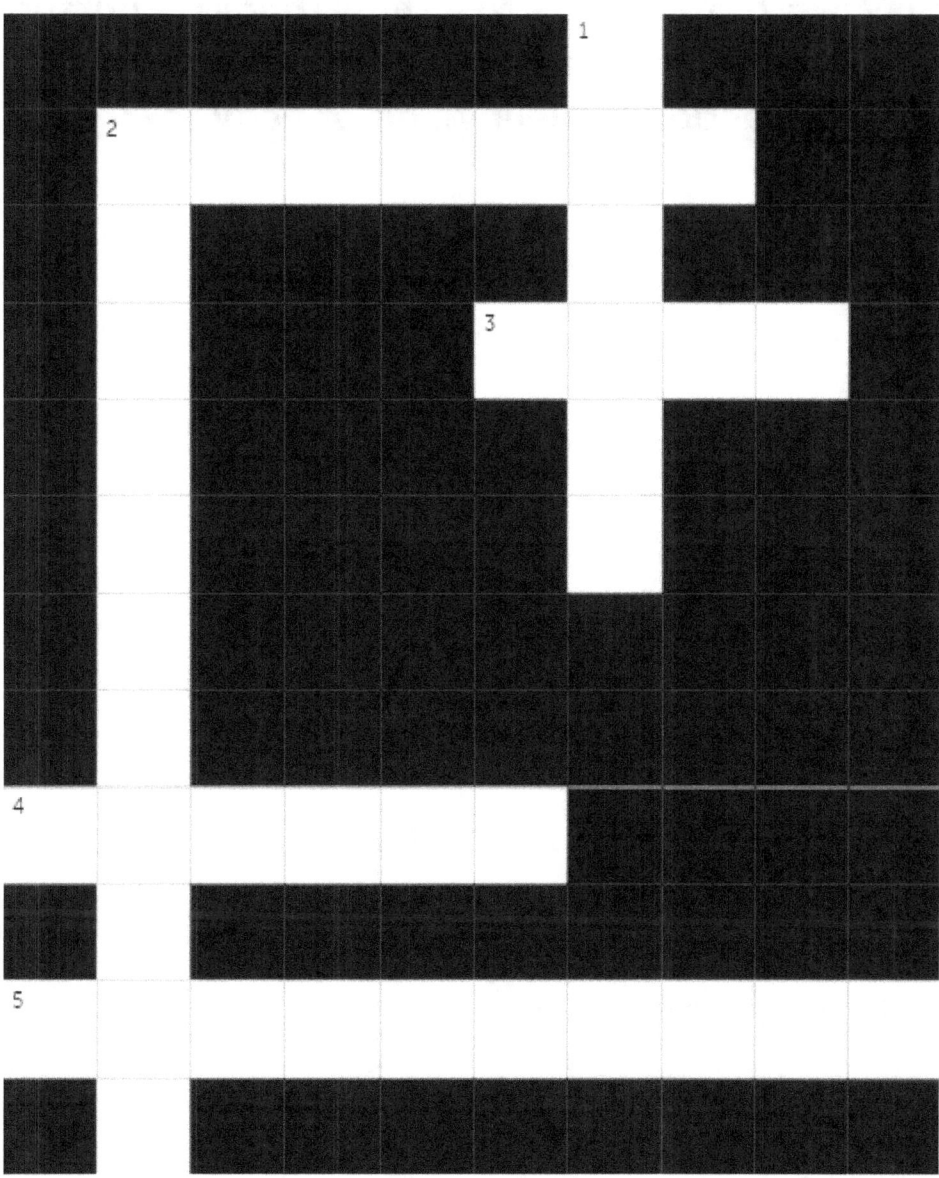

Across

2) By the time I got my Master's I was already considered a _____ of conceptual photography.

3) As time went on, I started using _____ and video in my works.

4) I'm known for using the _____ as a catalyst.

5) My signature technique is _____.

Down

1) I was the first African American woman to exhibit at the _____ Biennale

2) I'm mostly known for powerful artwork that combine _____ with words

Directions: Write the correct noun in each sentence.

A noun is a word that refers to a thing (book), a person (Betty Crocker), an animal (cat), a place (Omaha), an idea (justice), or an action (yodeling). bit of body text

exploration	canvas	sculptor	camera	instinct
depth	conviction	museum	painting	dedication
portrait	exhibition	realm	gallery	Imagery
passion	scenery			

1) Life is a great big _____ and you should throw all the paint on it you can.

2) The national grassland _____ of Little Missouri is unrivalled.

3) Water was found at a _____ of 30 meters.

4) African vases are disposed around the _____.

5) The seller took the _____ down from the wall.

6) Many of my works use culture _____.

7) Journalists will be able to preview the _____ tomorrow.

8) Italian bowls are disposed around the _____.

9) Painting is silent _____ and poetry is a speaking picture.

10) My friend turned the _____ on and stood beside her.

Directions: Unscramble the words below about Lorna. See if you can get the bonus word.

					9	8				
1										
2						6				
3							4			
4	1									
5										
6			7				3			
7				5						
8										
9										
10			2							
11								10		

BONUS WORD

1	2	3	4	5	6	7	8	9	10

Unscramble Words

1) ctouginn **2)** lnensecki **3)** hrgeimtna **4)** rcororid

5) rsp9op **6)** easvbeonlsem **7)** tsaeed **8)** puosceclda

9) bastske **10)** abrbraa

9

Directions: This is the WGLT Challenge. Solve the cryptogram. As the puzzle solver, you need to find which number belongs to which character. And this can be pretty challenging! You will need to match the number with the letter. There are some letters given to you below. This will help you solve the other words and unlock more characters. **Good Luck.**

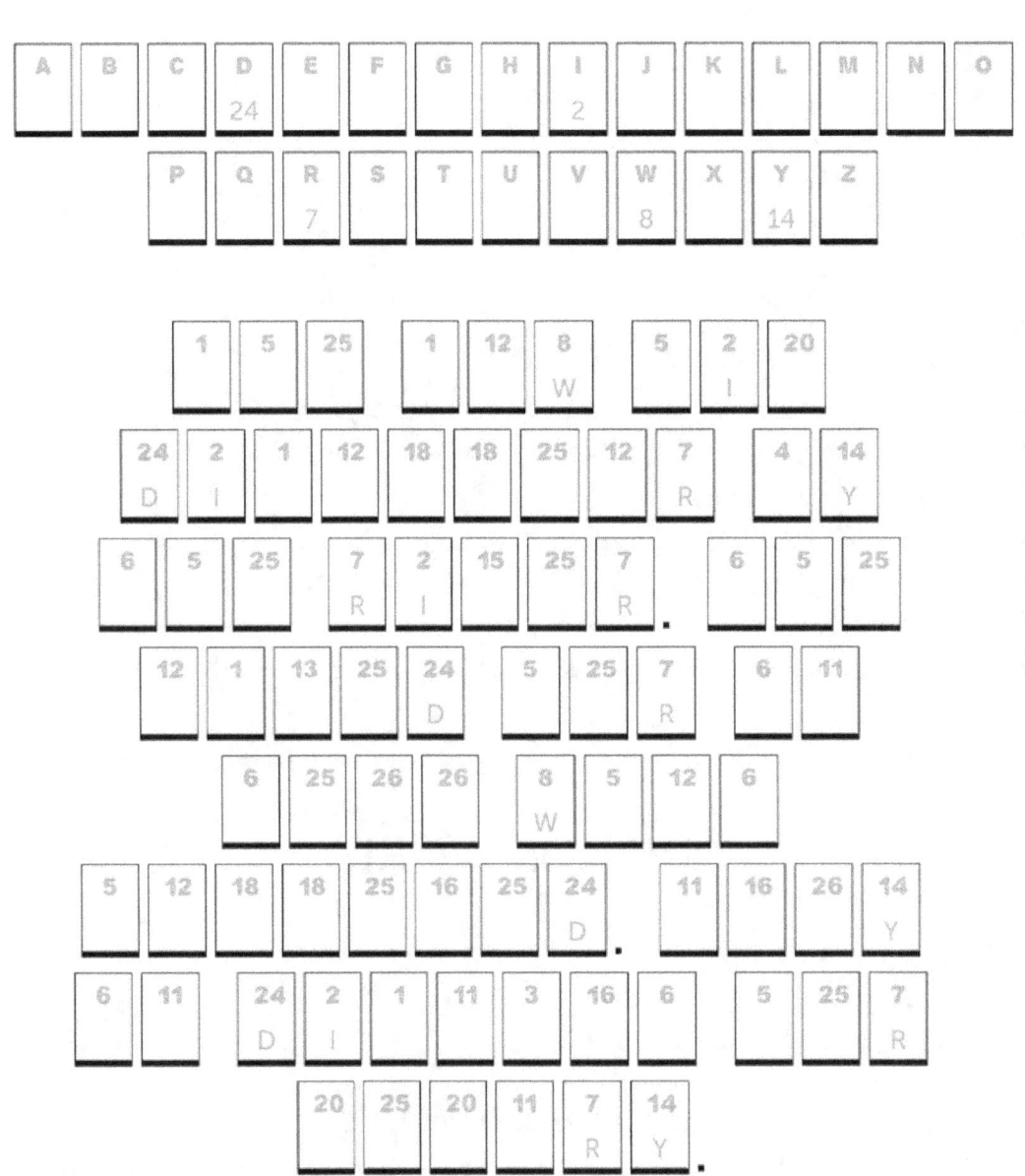

Michael S Harper

Michael S. Harper

March 18, 1938 – May 7, 2016
POET

11

Michael S Harper

Michael S Harper

Michael S Harper

Michael S. Harper

Michael S. Harper

Michael S. Harper

Hi, my name is Michael S. Harper I was born on March 18, 1938, in Brooklyn, New York. I attended Los Angeles City College, where I earned my Bachelor of Arts and Master of Arts in English studies. One of the things that I'm best known for is blending poetry with jazz. Some of the poems that I'm known for are "Nightmare Begins Responsibility," "Honorable Amendments," and "Double Take." I taught English at Contra Costa College in San Pablo, CA, after entering the U.S. Poetry Prize Competition and losing. The support and backing of Gwendolyn Brooks inspired me to keep going. Soon after, I published my first book, "Dear John, Dear Coltrane".

1. Where was I born?
   A. Brooklyn, NY
   B. Orlando, FL
   C. Portland, OR
2. Who inspired me to publish my first book?
   A. W.B Yeats
   B. Gwendolyn Brooks
   C. Sylvia Plath
3. What is my Master of Arts degree in?
   A. Poetry
   B. Medical
   C. English

Directions: Find the words associated with Michael's life and career.

B	B	L	A	C	K	H	I	S	T	O	R	Y	C	O	X
V	R	N	D	M	F	K	Y	H	X	Q	Q	U	W	Z	M
P	I	O	I	U	C	J	A	Z	Z	Q	L	Z	S	L	T
J	O	C	W	V	N	Z	P	N	W	T	K	E	D	U	G
L	X	E	D	N	Y	T	A	D	U	J	I	O	R	U	X
N	P	P	T	L	U	G	S	R	Q	D	S	O	A	I	G
K	Q	N	I	L	R	N	E	G	U	P	S	Y	J	V	D
T	W	M	R	H	A	L	I	T	H	N	F	O	P	N	R
H	A	N	K	Q	Q	U	S	V	E	Y	R	T	E	O	P
F	Y	F	Z	D	P	H	R	W	E	X	D	D	J	M	X
Z	F	N	A	T	S	S	Y	E	L	R	K	R	M	U	E
J	I	Z	Y	I	Y	O	T	H	A	X	S	B	D	G	Q
W	N	D	L	P	R	D	O	I	P	T	F	I	C	H	Q
X	X	G	A	K	R	N	S	X	O	B	E	B	T	G	P
Q	N	G	E	J	W	F	E	M	V	E	W	U	F	Y	Z
E	K	X	B	R	O	O	K	L	Y	N	Q	N	H	N	W

Find These Words

NEWYORK	BROWNUNIVERSITY	JAZZ
POETRY	CULTURE	FAMILY
BLACKHISTORY	ENGLISHSTUDIES	BROOKLYN
POETLAUREATE		

15

A poem's form refers to its structure: elements like its line lengths and meters, stanza lengths, rhyme schemes (if any) and systems of repetition. Every poem has a form—its own way of approaching these elements—whether that form is unique just to that poem, or part of a more widely used poetic form.

1) Which element is not a poem's form?
A. Rhyme schemes
B. Style
C. Length
D. Systems of repetition

2) What is a poems form?
A. Refers to its design
B. Refers to its structure
C. Refers to its frame
D. Refers to its texture

3) Every poem has a_____?
A. Profile
B. Formation
C. Form
D. Outline

Directions: Read and answer the questions below. There are clues in the puzzle to help you. Try and solve the cryptic message.

Clue for cryptic message: Michael used this in some of his poetry.

1) _____ is a poem that tells a story, usually (but not always) in four-line stanzas called quatrains.

2) _____ is a form of poetry that typically reflects on death or loss.

3) _____ is a highly structured poem made up of five tercets followed by a quatrain, with two repeating rhymes and two refrains.

4) _____ is a long, often book-length, narrative in verse form that retells the heroic journey of a single person or a group of persons.

5) _____ is a poem that consists of five lines in a single stanza with a rhyme scheme of AABBA.

6) _____ is a style of lyric poetry that usually features intense emotion or a vivid image of nature.

7) _____ is a complex, thirty-nine-line poem featuring the intricate repetition of end-words in six stanzas and an envoi.

8) _____ is a fourteen line poem with a fixed rhyme scheme.

9) _____ is a poem where certain letters in each line spell out a word or phrase.

10) _____ is a short lyric poem that praises an individual, an idea, or an event.

11) _____ is the name given to poetry that doesn't use any strict meter or rhyme scheme.

12) _____ is how much is said in how little of space.

17

Directions: This is the WGLT Challenge. Solve the cryptogram. As the puzzle solver, you need to find which number belongs to which character. And this can be pretty challenging! You will need to match the number with the letter. There are some letters given to you below. This will help you solve the other words and unlock more characters. **Good Luck.**

Audre Lorde

Audre Lorde

February 18, 1934 – November 17, 1992
WRITER

19

LEFT BLANK ON PURPOSE

Audre Lorde

Audre Lorde

Audre Lorde

Audre Lorde

Audre Lorde

Audre Lorde

Hi, my name is Audrey Lorde, although I'm better known as Audre Lorde. I was born on February 18, 1934, in Harlem, New York, NY. I chose to drop the "y" from my first name while still a child, explaining in her book "Zami: A New Spelling of My Name" that she was more interested in the artistic symmetry of the "e"-endings in the two side-by-side names "Audre Lorde" than in spelling her name the way her parents had intended. I attended Hunter College High School, which is a secondary school for intellectually gifted students. I graduated from Hunter College, as well as Columbia University, with a master's degree in library science. One of the works that I'm best known for is Kitchen Table: Women of Color Press. Some of the poems that I wrote include "From a Land Where Other People Live," "Coal," "The Black Unicorn," and "A Burst of Light." I'm also known as "Gamba Adisa," which means "Warrior: She Who Makes Her Meaning Known."

1. Which poem is not mine?
   A. Coal
   B. Notes of a Native Son
   C. The Black Unicorn
2. What does Gamba Adisa mean?
   A. Warrior
   B. Soldier
   C. Gladiator
3. Where was I born?
   A. Brooklyn, NY
   B. Harlem, New York, NY
   C. Columbus, OH

Directions: Answer the questions, to solve the crossword puzzle. You can use the internet if you get stuck on any question.

Across

1) My first published poem appeared in _____ magazine.

5) My book Coal _____ of five various layers of my identity.

7) Gambda Adisa, for _____: She Who Makes Her Meaning Known.

8) My Staten Island home is an official New York City _____.

Down

1) I was a breast cancer _____.

2) I co-founded a publishing company called _____ Table: Women of Color Press.

3) The Black _____ is consider to be my greatest poetic work.

4) I became a _____ to gain tools for ordering and analyzing information.

6) I use to speak in _____ literally.

Directions: Read the text below. Then answer the questions that follow.

A lot of poets use a **thesaurus** when they want to use a different word. A thesaurus is a book of words or of information about a particular field or set of concepts especially : a book of words and their **synonyms** and **antonyms**. In each row underline the word that doesn't belong.

1) structure   design   network   disorganization

2) craft   art   inability   technique

3) prose   song   poems   verse

4) ebony   onyx   milky   black

5) future   past   history   yesterday

6) cadence   rhythm   prose   tune

7) gap   solid   void   blank

8) statue   picture   original   illustration

9) melody   song   tune   silence

10) simile   dissimilarity   analogy   metaphor

Directions: Unscramble the words below about Audre. See if you can get the bonus word.

	1	2	3	4	5	6	7	8	9	10	11	12	13	14	15	16	17

Unscramble Words

1) jtsunescii   **2)** wrroira   **3)** eotp

4) bnrraiial   **5)** mzia   **6)** nbailse

7) nraecc   **8)** klbca   **9)** trerwi

10) otmrhe   **11)** oirnsyaiv   **12)** ealfme

25

Directions: This is the WGLT Challenge. Solve the cryptogram. As the puzzle solver, you need to find which number belongs to which character. And this can be pretty challenging! You will need to match the number with the letter. There are some letters given to you below. This will help you solve the other words and unlock more characters. **Good Luck.**

James Baldwin

James Baldwin

August 2, 1924 – December 1, 1987
WRITER

27

LEFT BLANK ON PURPOSE

James Baldwin

James Baldwin

James Baldwin

James Baldwin

James Baldwin

Hi, my name is James Baldwin. I was born on August 2, 1924, in Harlem, New York, NY. I attended DeWitt Clinton High School. I worked on the school's magazine, The Magpie. Some of the poems that I'm known for include "Notes of a Native Son," "Giovanni's Room," "Go Tell It on the Mountain," and "The Fire Next Time." I was a voice for the American civil rights movement. I moved to Paris, France, when I was 24 to escape the prejudice against Black people in the US. I wanted to be known for my work and not merely as a Negro writer. I returned to the US several years later and joined the Congress of Racial Equality (CORE). I traveled and lectured about racial inequality.

1. How old was I when I moved to Paris?
   A. 27
   B. 24
   C. 30
2. What was the name of my High School Magazine?
   A. The Gazette
   B. The New Yorker
   C. The Magpie
3. Which work of art is not my own?
   A. Notes of a Native Son
   B. Still I Rise
   C. Giovanni's Room

Directions: Find the words associated with James life and career.

V	J	W	F	W	H	P	U	V	N	V	S	U	K
S	L	E	C	N	A	S	S	I	A	N	E	R	X
H	O	J	M	G	V	F	Z	F	W	N	K	S	S
A	P	D	C	R	I	T	I	C	Q	T	K	Y	K
R	R	A	Q	F	Y	E	L	D	J	Y	M	T	T
L	E	N	C	O	X	R	W	F	D	I	B	I	N
E	H	D	V	T	R	E	T	I	R	W	R	L	S
M	C	B	E	T	I	T	Y	E	R	Z	H	A	G
P	A	Q	S	G	J	V	L	D	O	N	F	U	Y
F	E	E	Q	S	Z	M	I	L	F	P	J	Q	D
A	R	Q	O	I	Y	X	M	S	I	R	F	E	A
Z	P	E	S	M	E	A	A	R	T	S	W	P	V
Y	G	U	N	R	P	Z	F	Z	H	F	L	U	C
D	L	C	W	E	R	A	W	P	A	R	I	S	N

PREACHER	WRITER	CRITIC
ACTIVIST	POETRY	FAMILY
HARLEM	PARIS	EQUALITY
RENAISSANCE		

Directions: Read the text below. Then answer the questions that follow. Let's learn about continents. A **continent** is one of Earth's seven main divisions of land. The continents are, from largest to smallest: **Asia**, **Africa**, **North America**, **South America**, **Antarctica**, **Europe** and **Australia**. James was able to visit four continents while he was alive. **Here are some of the places. Lets see if you can match it to the right continent. Draw a line to the correct continent. A continent may have more than one answer.**

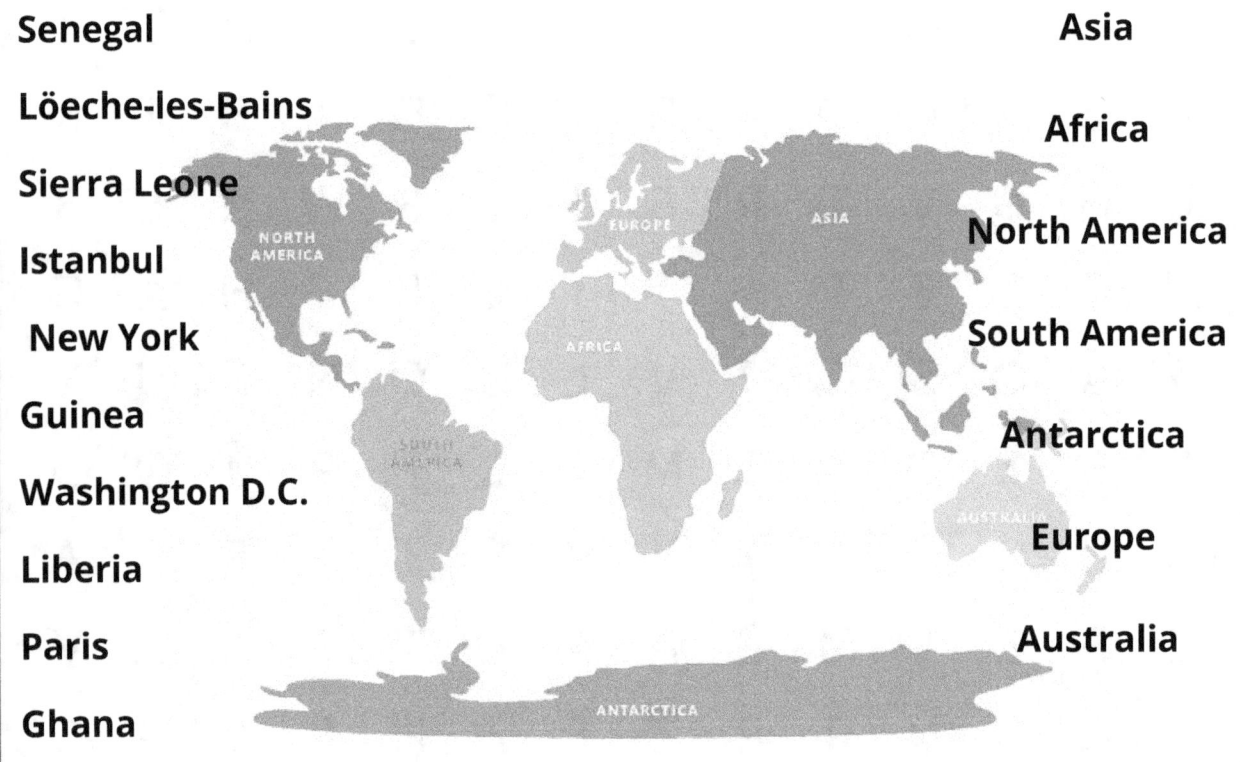

Senegal   **Asia**

Löeche-les-Bains

Sierra Leone   **Africa**

Istanbul   **North America**

 New York   **South America**

Guinea   **Antarctica**

Washington D.C.

Liberia   **Europe**

Paris   **Australia**

Ghana

1) What continent do you live on?

2) What city or town do you live in?

3) How many people live in your city or town?

4) Name three countries and cities or towns you would love to visit?

Directions: Read and answer the questions below. These are the different forms of poetry. There are clues in the puzzle to help you. Try and solve the cryptic message.

Clue for cryptic message: James was a big advocate for this movement.

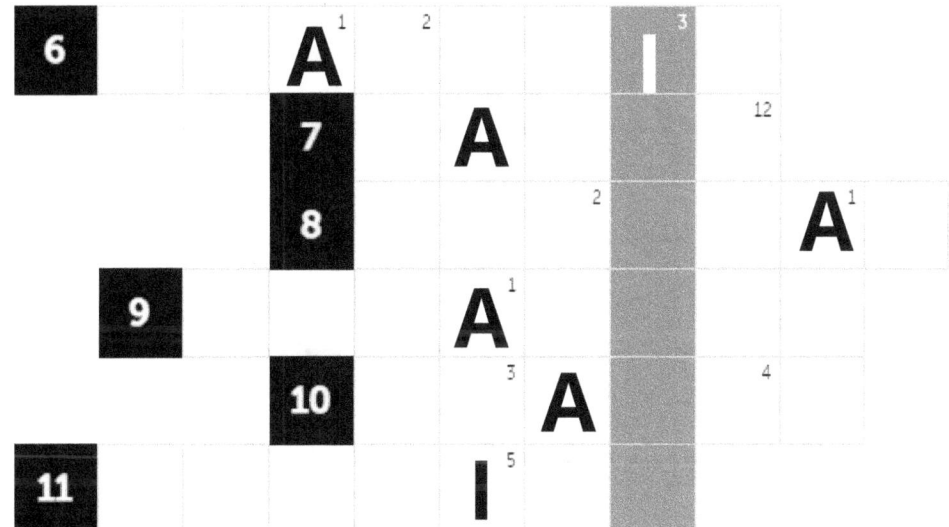

1) I worked as a film _____.
2) My first novel was Go Tell it on the _____.
3) I have written over five _____ in my life.
4) My first essay collection, Notes of a _____ son was published in 1955.
5) I wrote a _____ before I was eleven.
6) American Harlem Renaissance painter _____ Delaney was my mentor.
7) I moved to _____, to keep from going to jail or being killed.
8) I attended Frederick _____ Junior High school.
9) I was a _____ during my teen years.
10) I was known as an _____.
11) I have published over 15 short _____.

Directions: This is the WGLT Challenge. Solve the cryptogram. As the puzzle solver, you need to find which number belongs to which character. And this can be pretty challenging! You will need to match the number with the letter. There are some letters given to you below. This will help you solve the other words and unlock more characters. **Good Luck.**

Augusta Savage

Augusta Savage

February 29, 1892 – March 27, 1962
SCULPTOR

35

LEFT BLANK ON PURPOSE

Augusta Savage

Augusta Savage

Augusta Savage

Augusta Savage

Augusta Savage

Augusta Savage

Hi, my name is Augusta Savage. I was born on February 29, 1892, in Green Cove Springs, FL. I attended The Cooper Union in NY. I obtained my first commission from the New York Public Library. I created a sculpture of W.E.B. Du Bois. I'm best known for creating works that have elevated images of Black culture into the mainstream American consciousness. Some of my works are Gamin, The Tom Tom, Envy and Marcus Garvey. I traveled to France to attend the Academie de la Grande Chaumiere, which is a leading Parisian art school. I returned a few years later to the US, where I became the first African American artist to be elected to the National Association of Women Painters and Sculptors. I was also a central figure in the Harlem Renaissance.

1. What state was I born in?
   A. Texas
   B. Florida
   C. Ohio
2. What was the name of my work for my first commission?
   A. Marcus Garvey
   B. Gamin
   C. W.E.B. Du Bois
3. Which work of art is mine?
   A. The Tom Tom
   B. Sadness
   C. Head of a Negro Boy

Directions: Answer the questions, to solve the crossword puzzle. You can use the internet if you get stuck on any question.

Across

6) Most of my work was made with clay or _____.

7) I exhibited and twice won awards, at the _____ Salon

8) I worked for _____ rights for African Americans in the arts.

Down

1) Harlem Renaissance was an African-American _____ movement centered out of Harlem.

2) I was associated with the Harlem_____.

3) During The Great _____ I launched the Savage Studio of Arts and Crafts.

4) My sculpture The _____ was inspired by the inspirational national Black anthem.

5) _____ is a French word that means "Street Urchin." This is one of my more popular sculptures.

Directions: Read the text below. Then answer the questions that follow.

The task here is to read each definition and then place the materials in the right Colum. **Additive sculpting** processes involve adding materials to "build up" the sculpture. **Subtractive sculpting** processes rely on the removal of the material to "reveal" the sculpture. These materials are used to make sculptures.

Additive sculpting   **Subtractive sculpting**

Model Magic is made by Crayola. It is a non-toxic and inexpensive sculpting material that air dries.

Soap is a great material for carving.

Plasticine clay is colored, oil-based clay.

Plaster of Paris is inexpensive and easy to mix. Pour it into empty paper milk cartons.

Balsa wood is soft and pliable. It's extremely easy to carve.

Air Dry Clay can be very inexpensive, non-toxic and can be painted when its dry.

Polymer clay is actually PVC. Liquid is added to make it pliable enough to be formed and shaped.

Directions: Unscramble the words below about Augusta. See if you can get the bonus word.

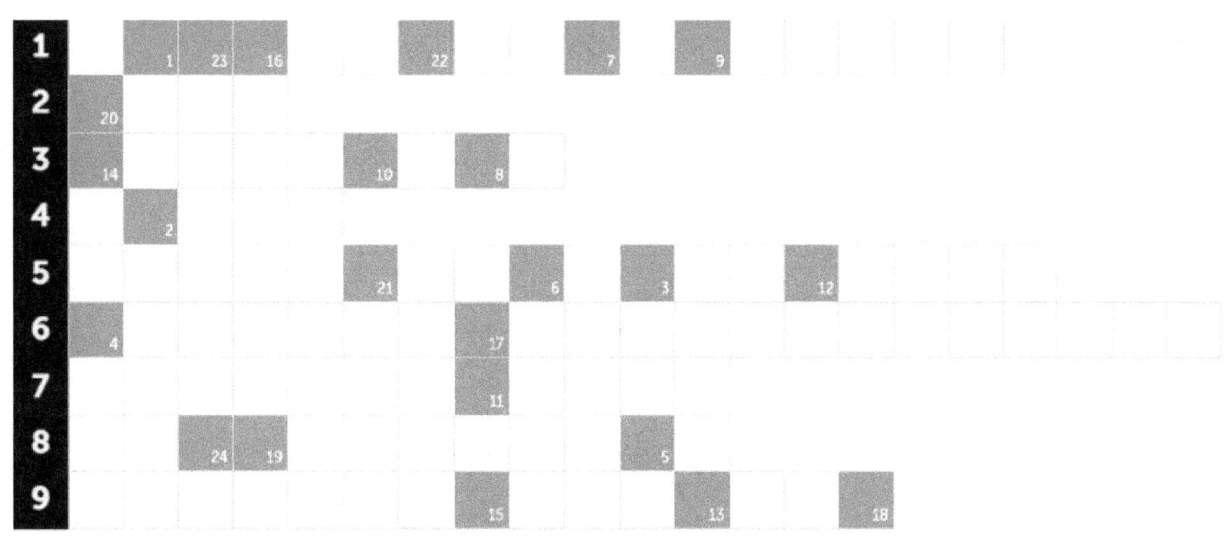

BONUS WORD

Unscramble Words

1) anttedocasathmrba

2) eyvn

3) thetmomto

4) amnig

5) fnraowniaiqtumomae

6) sirtevlgnideyieovfnca

7) .osbue.dwb.i

8) aryvuescmgra

9) hiwygndgeltkonn

Directions: This is the WGLT Challenge. Solve the cryptogram. As the puzzle solver, you need to find which number belongs to which character. And this can be pretty challenging! You will need to match the number with the letter. There are some letters given to you below. This will help you solve the other words and unlock more characters. **Good Luck.**

A	B	C	D	E	F	G	H	I	J	K	L	M	N	O
18						13	1				5			

P	Q	R	S	T	U	V	W	X	Y	Z
						25				

1	15	18	25	23		10	19	23	18	4	23	16
I		A	V						A			

24	17	4	15	1	24	13		19	23	18	5	5	11
				I		G				A	L	L	

12	23	18	9	4	1	20	9	5
		A			I			L

,

19	23	18	5	5	11	5	18	2	4	1	24	13
		A	L	L		L	A			I		G

,

12	9	4	1	20	1	10	18	24
			I		I		A	

1	24	2	26	1	19	23	17	24	23	17	20
I				I							

4	15	23	2	23

11	17	9	24	13	2	4	23	19	2		4	17
				G								

16	23	25	23	5	17	26		4	15	23
V		L								

4	18	5	23	24	4		1	3	24	17	21
	A	L					I				

4	15	23	11	26	17	2	2	23	2	2

,

4	15	23	24	8	11

8	17	24	9	8	23	24	4	21	1	5	5
									I	L	L

12	23	1	24	4	15	23	1	19	21	17	19	3
		I					I					

.

42

Amiri Baraka

Amiri Baraka

October 7, 1934 – January 9, 2014
WRITER/POET

43

Amiri Baraka

Amiri Baraka

Amiri Baraka

Amiri Baraka

Amiri Baraka

Amiri Baraka

Hi, my name is Everett Jones, but I changed my name to Amiri Baraka after the assassination of Malcolm X. I left the apolitical movement in favor of addressing racial politics. I was born on October 7, 1934, in Newark, NJ. I attended Barringer High School and graduated with a bachelor's degree in English from Howard University. One of the things that I'm best known for is being a major force in the Black Arts Movement. Some of the poems that I'm known for are "The Dead Lecturer," Transbluesency: The Selected Poetry of Amiri Baraka/LeRoi Jones (1961–1995) and "Dutchman." I also joined the Air Force in 1954 as a gunner. I reached the rank of sergeant during my enlistment.

1. Who's assassination caused me change my name?
   A. Martin Luther King Jr
   B. Malcolm X
   C. Medgar Evers
2. What was the name of my High School?
   A. Ross High School
   B. DeWitt Clinton High School
   C. Barringer High School
3. Which rank was I in the military?
   A. Sergeant Major
   B. Sergeant First Class
   C. Sergeant

Directions: Find the words associated with Amiri's life and career.

```
F  B  C  M  Y  U  G  E  N  H  F  J  G  L  Z  F  A  L
Q  L  O  F  B  E  A  T  P  O  E  T  S  Q  B  C  F  P
M  A  L  C  A  L  I  D  R  V  L  F  K  I  J  W  R  G
T  C  U  O  B  B  D  U  R  P  E  V  H  M  R  C  I  E
H  K  M  M  V  K  R  T  A  M  M  A  K  E  J  U  C  Y
E  A  B  M  G  N  A  C  B  W  E  N  T  C  B  M  A  E
B  R  I  U  Y  Q  W  H  B  T  H  I  O  G  N  A  N  R
O  T  A  N  D  X  O  M  I  P  R  T  L  W  O  M  S  H
O  S  U  I  A  P  H  A  G  W  T  E  O  P  Q  I  T  J
K  M  N  S  M  O  G  N  Y  S  M  Y  V  B  E  E  U  S
O  O  I  T  B  T  A  A  E  A  F  W  P  C  T  D  M
F  V  V  I  P  V  L  F  L  K  O  N  S  R  N  Q  I  I
M  E  E  U  T  P  N  C  Z  Z  N  F  O  R  Q  Z  E  O
O  M  R  O  K  J  O  J  H  S  M  F  E  N  U  B  S  S
N  E  S  N  A  L  O  P  S  O  R  U  R  V  Y  S  S  Z
K  N  I  W  M  X  W  T  N  I  K  C  A  K  C  U  A  N
V  T  T  X  W  L  F  H  A  R  R  Q  Q  Y  M  O  S  X
U  N  Y  H  V  U  T  Y  K  L  R  C  O  D  E  P  C  B
```

Find These Words

POET

COLUMBIAUNIVERSITY

MALCOLMX

AFRICANSTUDIES

BEATPOETS

PLAYWRITER

YUGEN

IMAMU

HOWARD

COMMUNIST

AIRFORCE

DUTCHMAN

BLACKARTSMOVEMENT

THEBOOKOFMONK

Directions: Read the text below. Then answer the questions that follow.

Create a possessive phrase using an apostrophe. **Add 's** after a singular noun or a plural noun **that doesn't end with s**. **Add '** after a plural noun **that ends with s**.

Amiri – books   _____

teachers – papers   _____

Obalaji – canvas   _____

student – pencil   _____

friends – jacket   _____

Rewrite the sentence using possessive nouns. Example in red.
The bike belongs to Sam. It is Sam's bike. The eggs belong to the chickens. They are the chickens' eggs.

The pants belong to Sue.   _____

The flute belongs to the Jones.   _____

The hat belongs to the doll.   _____

The library belongs to the Barakas. _____

The mask belongs to Kellie.   _____

The sandals belong to Lisa.   _____

48

Directions: Read and answer the questions below. These are the different forms of poetry. There are clues in the puzzle to help you. Try and solve the cryptic message.

Clue for cryptic message: This is one of Amari's poems he created.

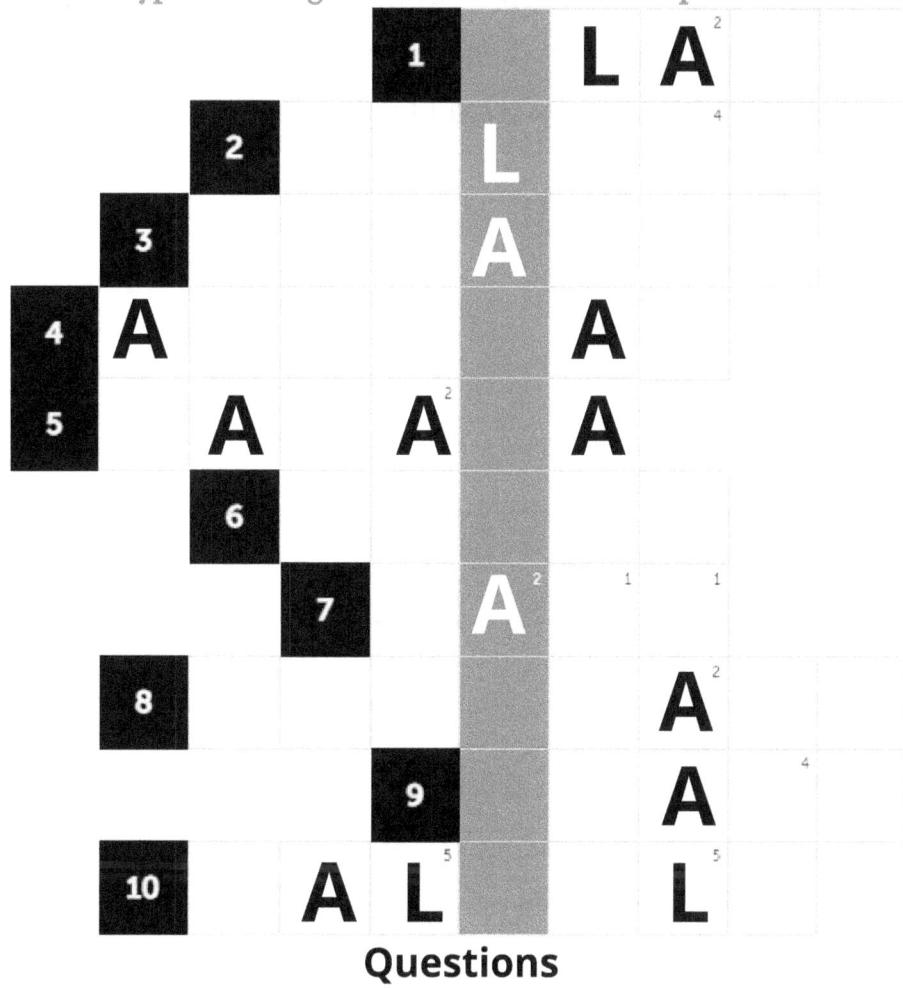

Questions

2) Preface to a Twenty _____ Suicide Note was my first major collection of poetry.

3) I helped found the New York Poets _____.

4) I was a professor of _____ Studies at Stony Brook University.

5) I changed my name from Leroi Jones to Amiri _____.

6) I taught a course entitled "Black _____ and Their Fictions".

7) One of my most notable poems is "The Music: Reflection on ____ and Blues".

8) I was a ____ in the U.S. Air Force.

9) _____ is a Swahili title for "spiritual leader".

10) After _____ X's assassination, I changed my name.

49

Directions: This is the WGLT Challenge. Solve the cryptogram. As the puzzle solver, you need to find which number belongs to which character. And this can be pretty challenging! You will need to match the number with the letter. There are some letters given to you below. This will help you solve the other words and unlock more characters. **Good Luck.**

50

Gwendolyn Brooks

Gwendolyn Brooks

June 7, 1917 – December 3, 2000
POET/ARTHOR

51

LEFT BLANK ON PURPOSE

Gwendolyn Brooks

Gwendolyn Brooks

Gwendolyn Brooks

Gwendolyn Brooks

Gwendolyn Brooks

Gwendolyn Brooks

Hi, my name is Gwendolyn Brooks. I was born on June 7, 1917, in Topeka, KS but moved to Chicago, IL during the Great Migration. I graduated from Englewood High School. One of the things that I'm best known for is being the first African American poet to win the Pulitzer Prize. I was also named the poet laureate of Illinois. Some of the poems that I'm known for are "The Children of the Poor," "Sadie and Maud," "The Mother," and "To Be in Love." I also was the U.S. Poet Laureate for the 1985–86 term. I was also the first African American woman to be inducted into the American Academy of Arts and Letters. I'm also on the commemorative postage stamp that was issued by the USPS in 2012.

1. What year did I become U.S. Poet Laureate?
   A. 1987
   B. 1985
   C. 1986
2. In what city did I grow up?
   A. Topeka
   B. Chicago
   C. Tampa
3. What award was I the first to win?
   A. Poetry London Prize
   B. Pulitzer Prize
   C. Alice James Award

Directions: Answer the questions, to solve the crossword puzzle. You can use the internet if you get stuck on any question.

Across

1) When I was seventeen the _____ Defender published my poems.

3) President _____ invited me to read at a Library of Congress poetry festival in 1962.

4) Some of my poetry styles were sonnets, free verse and _____.

6) I use to work for the National Association of the _____ of Colored People.

7) I taught poetry at _____ College Chicago.

Down

2) My close friends called me _____.

5) I was born in _____ not Illinois.

6) My book _____ Allen helped me win the Pulitzer Prize for Poetry.

Directions: Read the text below. Then answer the questions that follow.

Lets learn about one of Gwendolyn styles of poetry which is a **ballad**. A **ballad** tells a story in a series of quatrains. Quatrains are four-line stanzas that often have a set rhyme scheme. **Ballads** are an ancient poetic form and early poets wrote them to be sung instead of read. They have a musical quality that makes reading them a joy. Some **ballads** also include a refrain that is repeated. The **ballad** is divided into stanzas, each with four lines, which is also known as a quatrain. The rhyme scheme can be ABAB or ABCB, which means that the second and fourth lines always rhyme together.

Write the letter of the word from the word bank that completes each sentence.

A) four   **B)** naturally   **C)** important   **D)** topic
 E) rhyme   **F)** attention   **G)** prose   **H)** senses

These are the steps to creating your own Ballad.

1) Choose a _____ for your Ballad.

2) Write your plot of the story as a _____ first. (Write your story without trying to make it _____ first.)

3) Choose what _format_ to build your Ballad.

4) Write your plot in groups of _____ lines.

5) The first line of your ballad is very _____. You need to capture the reader's _____ right away.

6) Use imagery, think about how you can describe things using your _____.

7) Read what you've wrote out loud. It should flow ____ and sound like a song.

Challenge: Now that you have the steps for a ballad. Lets try to write our own ballad.

Directions: Unscramble the words below about Gwendolyn. See if you can get the bonus word.

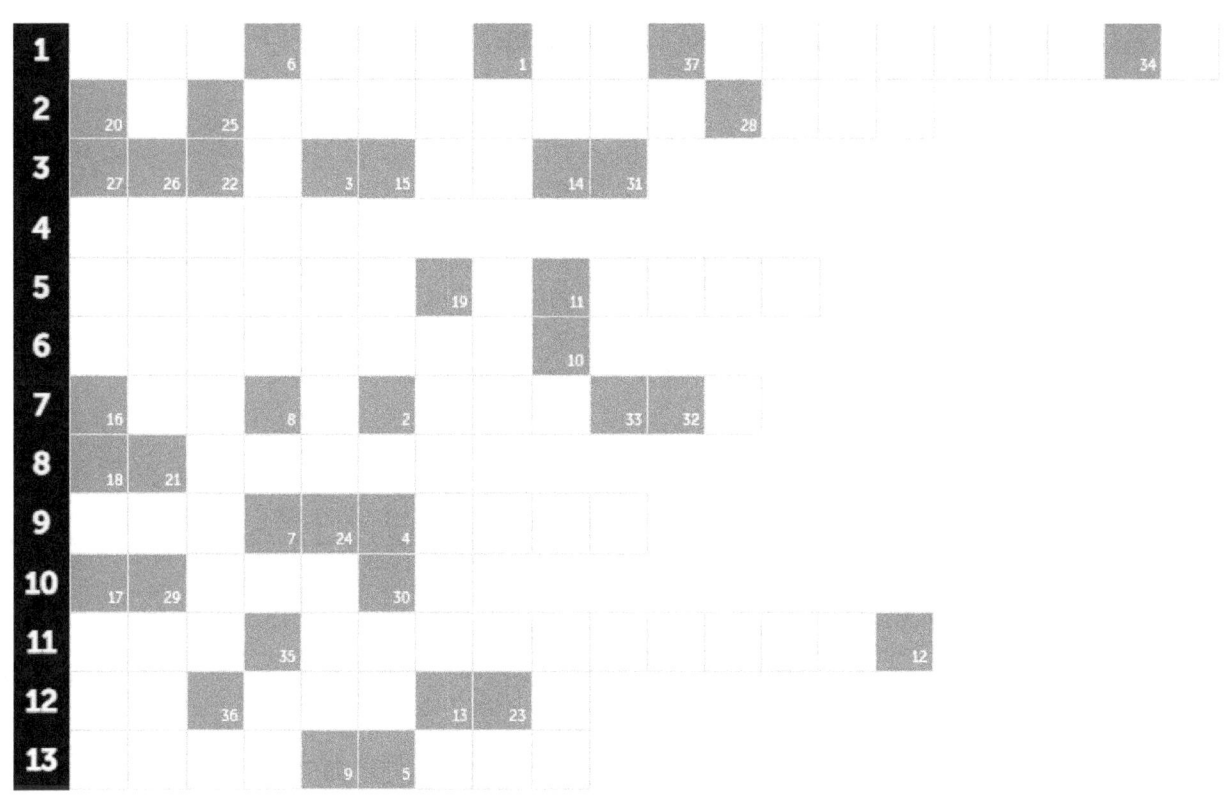

BONUS WORD

Unscramble Words

1) rivsbtonneatlelezeir

2) nfeecoeidrcagdh

3) dumaarmtah

4) aapcn

5) plptirzeureiz

6) mtreeohth

7) arpotleeateu

8) bsdllaa

9) naallnenie

10) ensonst

11) efniaalvsrtyrko

12) eeeesrvfr

13) leegnoodw

Directions: This is the WGLT Challenge. Solve the cryptogram. As the puzzle solver, you need to find which number belongs to which character. And this can be pretty challenging! You will need to match the number with the letter. There are some letters given to you below. This will help you solve the other words and unlock more characters. **Good Luck.**

A	B	C	D	E	F	G	H	I	J	K	L	M	N	O
9							11	7				16		

P	Q	R	S	T	U	V	W	X	Y	Z

8	11	21	17		10	15	18		18	19	21		14	11	21
	H													H	

14	21	6	16		16	7	17	15	6	7	14	10
			M		M	I				I		

15	6	16	7	17	15	6	7	14	7	21	19
		M	I				I		I		

7	17	6	21	23	21	6	21	17	2	21		14	15
I													

4	21	15	4	3	21		10	15	18		9	6	21
											A			,

14	21	3	3	7	17	25		14	11	21	16
				I					H		M

14	11	9	14		14	11	21	10		9	6	21
	H	A				H				A		

3	21	19	19	14	11	9	17
					H	A	

19	15	16	21	24	15	20	10		21	3	19	21
		M										

58

Gordon Parks

Gordon Parks

November 30, 1912 – March 7, 2006

PHOTOGRAPHER

59

Gordon Parks

Gordon Parks

Gordon Parks

Gordon Parks

Gordon Parks

Gordon Parks

Hi, my name is Gordon Parks. I was born on November 30, 1912, in Fort Scott, KS. I worked with the Farm Security Administration as a trainee under Roy Stryker, which produced one of my best-known photographs, American Gothic. One of the things that I'm best known for is photojournalism that reveals important aspects of American culture by focusing on issues of civil rights, poverty, race relations and urban life. Some of the images that I'm known for include Red Jackson, Emerging Man, Outside Looking In and Flavio Da Silva. I was also the first African American to direct a major motion picture, The Learning Tree. I also directed Shaft, Leadbelly and The Super Cops. In 1948, I became the staff photographer for Life magazine and the first African American to hold that position.

1. What is not one of the issues I focused on?
   A. civil rights
   B. fame
   C. urban life
2. What was the name of the Magazine I worked for?
   A. Time
   B. Life
   C. Ebony
3. Which film didn't I direct?
   A. Scarface
   B. Shaft
   C. The learning Tree

Directions: Find the words associated with Gordon's life and career.

M	W	R	S	H	A	F	T	O	X	J	E	W	E	P	U
M	P	B	A	T	E	C	H	N	I	Q	U	E	C	P	Y
B	N	A	Y	C	Q	B	Y	U	I	C	K	X	H	N	N
I	A	T	L	N	I	Z	G	M	Y	N	R	O	A	Q	Y
M	M	D	S	U	O	S	U	L	A	X	T	M	R	B	T
Q	G	E	Q	S	Y	B	M	Y	V	O	E	F	V	U	R
M	N	N	W	M	Q	Y	E	M	G	C	C	U	I	Y	E
R	I	O	X	L	E	O	G	R	N	C	G	W	M	M	V
B	G	R	F	I	V	O	A	A	L	D	T	R	M	J	O
J	R	W	R	F	P	P	S	L	F	U	K	T	C	A	P
V	E	J	A	C	H	S	K	N	I	P	S	X	R	Q	R
P	M	E	F	Y	I	W	L	K	F	T	S	E	R	B	W
C	E	Y	X	A	E	N	I	Z	G	A	M	E	F	I	L
J	O	G	N	D	X	U	L	W	C	A	X	N	G	E	B
K	S	E	O	S	D	N	B	J	C	K	Z	W	O	G	H
I	R	N	O	I	T	A	N	I	M	I	R	C	S	I	D

Find These Words

LIFEMAGZINE   CAMERA   RENAISSANCEMAN

FILMS   PHOTOGRAPHY   TECHNIQUE

SHAFT   EMERGINGMAN   EBONY

RACISM   POVERTY   DISCRIMINATION

Directions: Read the text below. Then answer the questions that follow.

Add a prefix to each base word to make a new word. Use **mis-, re-, un-, non-, over- or pre-**.

pre- means	before	re- means	again; back
mis- means	wrongly	un- means	opposite
non- means	not	over- means	too much

Example write   rewrite

view _____ do _____

write _____ judge _____

stick _____ cover _____

board _____ vent _____

specific _____ turn _____

place _____ lock _____

Challenge there are six of the prefix words **that you do or don't do during film processing what do you think they are.**

1. _____
2. _____
3. _____
4. _____
5. _____
6. _____

Directions: Read and answer the questions below. These are the different forms of poetry. There are clues in the puzzle to help you. Try and solve the cryptic message.

Clue for cryptic message: This is one of Gordan's films he directed.

Questions
1) I helped create the _____ genre in film.

2) I was the first African American photographer to work for _____ magazine.

3) I worked as a photographer in ____ for a couple years.

4) _____ Ellington was a hero of mine growing up.

5) In 1989, he composed a ___ dedicated to Martin Luther King.

6) I use to work for the Civilian _____ Corps.

7) In 1948, I was hired as a staff photographer for _____ magazine.

8) The _____ Tree was my first major film.

9) In 2002, he was inducted into the _____ Hall of Fame.

Directions: This is the WGLT Challenge. Solve the cryptogram. As the puzzle solver, you need to find which number belongs to which character. And this can be pretty challenging! You will need to match the number with the letter. There are some letters given to you below. This will help you solve the other words and unlock more characters. **Good Luck.**

Faith Ringgold

Faith Ringgold

October 8, 1930 – Present
PAINTER/WRITER

67

Faith Ringgold

Faith Ringgold

Faith Ringgold

Faith Ringgold

Faith Ringgold

Faith Ringgold

Hi, my name is Faith Ringgold. I was born on October 8, 1930, in Harlem, Manhattan, NY. I attended City College of New York. There, I received my bachelor's and master's degrees in art. One of the things that I'm best known for is my innovative quilted narrations. Some of the quilts that I created are called Street Story, Tar Beach 2, Somebody Stole My Broken Heart and Dancing at the Louvre. As an activist, I participated in several feminist and anti-racist organizations. Some of the groups that I participated in were the Women Artists in Revolution, the National Black Feminist Organization and the Black Arts Movement. I wrote and illustrated seventeen children's books, including Tar Beach, My Dream of Martin Luther King and Bonjour Lonnie.

1. What am I best know for?
   A. Children Books
   B. Art Work
   C. Quilts
2. How many children books have I published?
   A. 5
   B. 17
   C. 15
3. Which college did I attend?
   A. City College of New York
   B. Howard University
   C. New York University

Directions: Answer the questions, to solve the crossword puzzle. You can use the internet if you get stuck on any question.

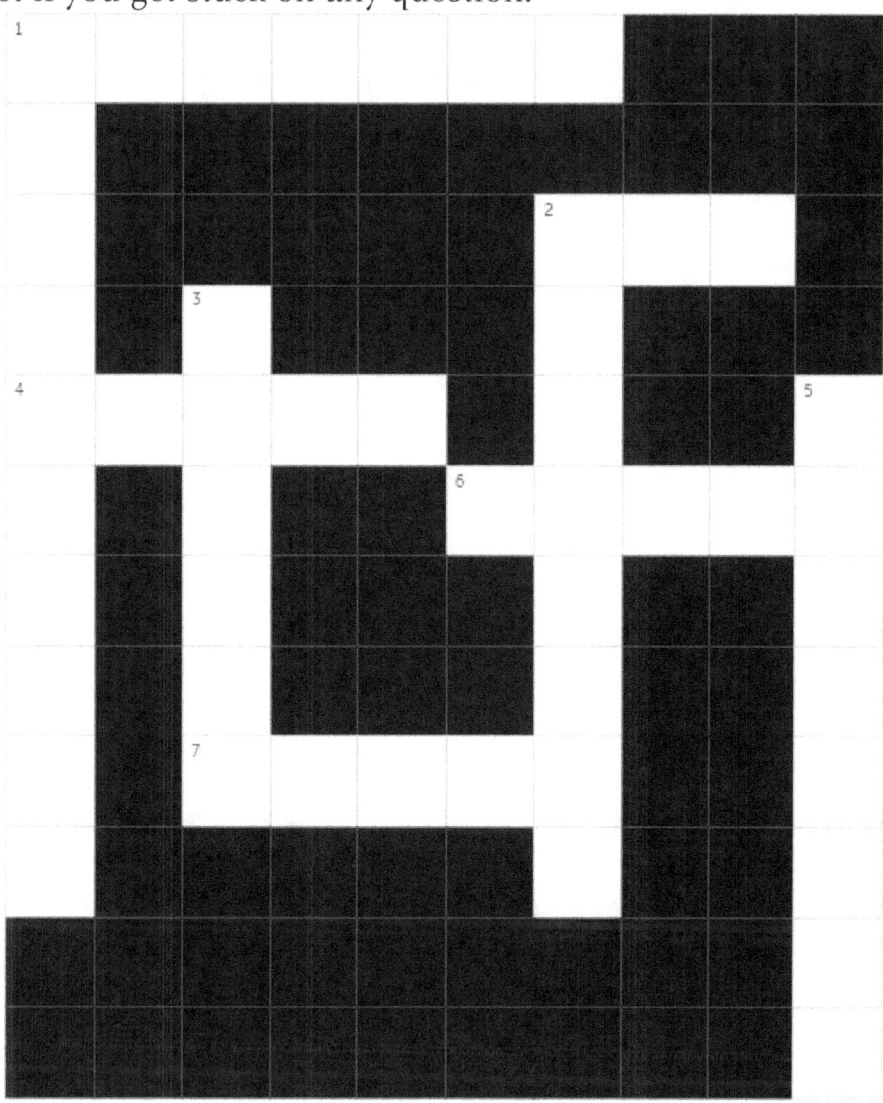

Across
1) I'm known for making _____ narrations on my beliefs.

2) I co-founded the AdHoc Women's _____ Committee.

4) I use to _____ art at the University of California, San Diego.

6) I have a sculpture series called the _____ mask series.

7) Tradition of _____ have been a great influence in my works.

Down
1) I have an app called _____ you can play on android or iphone.

2) I am an _____ for several feminist and anti-racist organizations.

3) My first quilt was called Echoes of _____.

5) Harlem Renaissance Party is one of my _____ books.

Directions: Read the text below. Then answer the questions that follow.

Prepositions tell us where or when something is. Common prepositions: **at, above, before, to, in, from**.

1)   Willi ordered a pizza for the family.

2)   I love going to the museum.

3)   We get on the bus every morning.

4)   I'm making a quilt for my mom.

5)   Andrew came from New York.

6)   My parents traveled out of town

7)   Are we heading to Europe?

8)   My brother bought some flowers for his niece.

9)   The doctor buys art for his patients.

10) I left my mask on the floor.

11) My mom helps me with quilts.

12) We picked the fabric off the ground.

Directions: Unscramble the words below about Faith. See if you can get the bonus word.

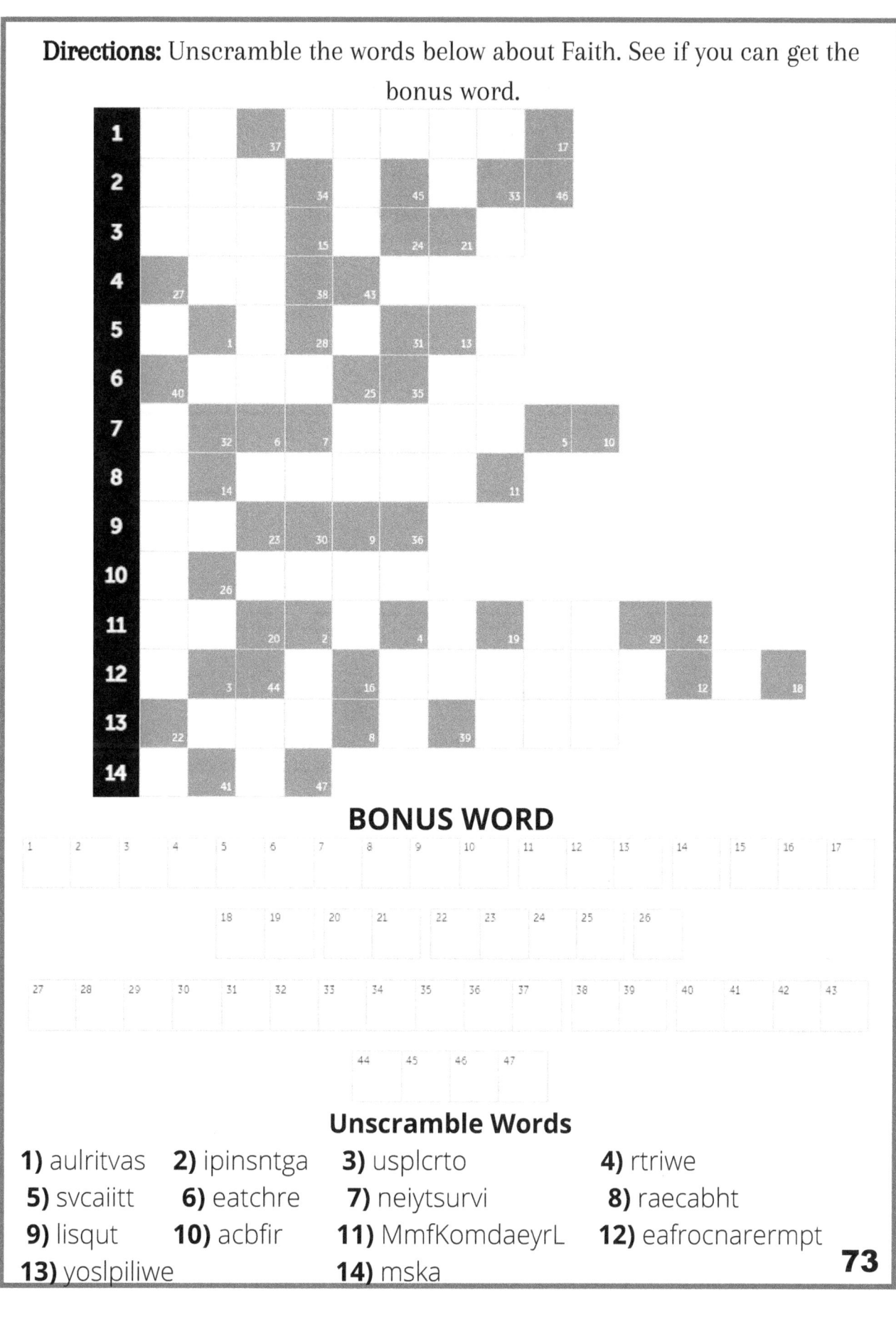

BONUS WORD

1	2	3	4	5	6	7	8	9	10	11	12	13	14	15	16	17

18	19	20	21	22	23	24	25	26

27	28	29	30	31	32	33	34	35	36	37	38	39	40	41	42	43

44	45	46	47

Unscramble Words

1) aulritvas **2)** ipinsntga **3)** usplcrto **4)** rtriwe

5) svcaiitt **6)** eatchre **7)** neiytsurvi **8)** raecabht

9) lisqut **10)** acbfir **11)** MmfKomdaeyrL **12)** eafrocnarermpt

13) yoslpiliwe **14)** mska

73

Directions: This is the WGLT Challenge. Solve the cryptogram. As the puzzle solver, you need to find which number belongs to which character. And this can be pretty challenging! You will need to match the number with the letter. There are some letters given to you below. This will help you solve the other words and unlock more characters. **Good Luck.**

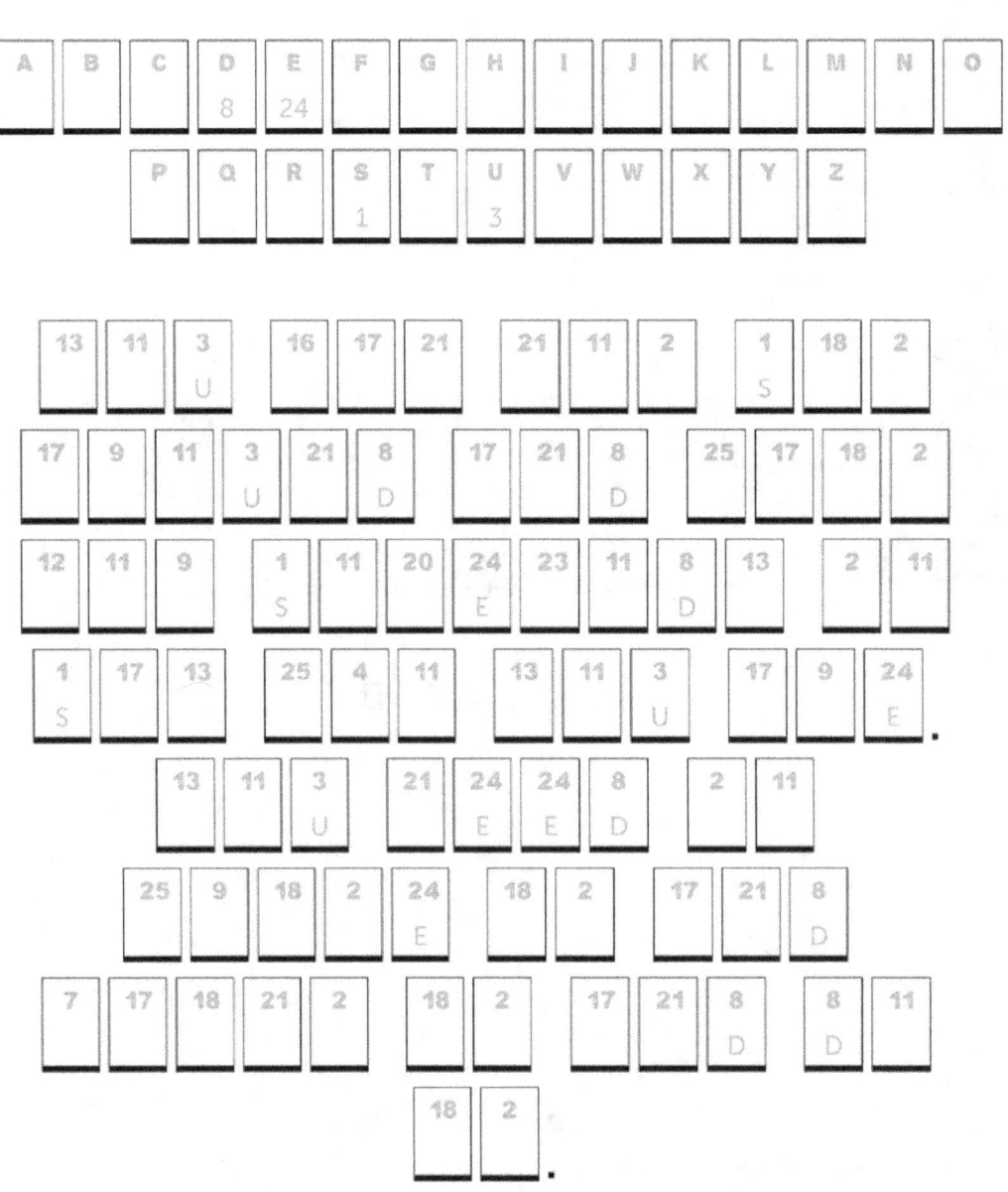

A	B	C	D	E	F	G	H	I	J	K	L	M	N	O
			8	24										

P	Q	R	S	T	U	V	W	X	Y	Z
			1		3					

13 11 3(U) 16 17 21 21 11 2 1(S) 18 2

17 9 11 3(U) 21 8(D) 17 21 8(D) 25 17 18 2

12 11 9 1(S) 11 20 24(E) 23 11 8(D) 13 2 11

1(S) 17 13 25 4 11 13 11 3(U) 17 9 24(E).

13 11 3(U) 21 24(E) 24(E) 8(D) 2 11

25 9 18 2 24(E) 18 2 17 21 8(D)

7 17 18 21 2 18 2 17 21 8(D) 8(D) 11

18 2.

Jacob Lawrence

Jacob Lawrence

September 7, 1917 – June 9, 2000
PAINTER

75

LEFT BLANK ON PURPOSE

Jacob Lawrence

Jacob Lawrence

Jacob Lawrence

Jacob Lawrence

Jacob Lawrence

Jacob Lawrence

Hi, my name is Jacob Lawrence. I was born on September 7, 1917, in Atlantic City, NJ. One of the things that I'm best known for is my modernist depictions of everyday life, as well as my epic narratives about African American history and historical figures. Some of the paintings that I'm known for are The Migration of the Negro, War Series, A Woman Mans a Cannon and Struggle. I was one of the few African American artists that the Metropolitan Museum of Art (the Met) recognized and featured in the museum. The piece that they featured was Pool Parlor, which they displayed in 1942. I was drafted by the U.S. Coast Guard during WWII and served as a public affairs specialist with the first racially integrated crew. I reached the rank of petty officer third class. I lived through the Great Migration, the Depression, the Jazz Age and the Harlem Renaissance. All of these events were inspirations for my work.

1. What year did the Met feature Pool Parlor?
   A. 1941
   B. 1942
   C. 1943
2. What was my rank in the US Coast Guard?
   A. Petty Officer First Class
   B. Petty Officer Third Class
   C. Petty Officer Second Class
3. What event helped influence some of my work of art?
   A. Franklin D Roosevelt getting elected to President
   B. The Depression
   C. World War I (WW I)

Directions: Find the words associated with Jacob's life and career.

T	T	I	F	W	Q	D	T	S	Y	H	S	G	M	Q	Z	D	P	A	B
O	X	H	B	F	D	J	O	F	T	W	V	E	J	D	Y	E	L	W	L
U	I	U	E	O	Q	T	H	E	Q	L	G	O	W	N	H	F	Y	S	A
S	H	S	Q	M	G	M	S	E	Q	T	H	N	A	W	T	B	S	L	C
S	D	E	P	L	I	N	A	C	E	N	E	M	L	N	J	A	U	A	K
A	Y	T	D	E	O	G	H	V	B	E	I	L	O	I	L	E	U	F	M
I	T	Y	K	C	W	U	R	R	A	C	U	T	E	G	Z	G	J	H	O
N	U	K	M	T	S	X	O	A	C	E	S	L	U	P	U	D	A	B	U
T	Y	H	V	N	H	W	D	U	T	L	I	O	R	S	O	R	F	H	N
L	E	U	S	S	N	M	B	R	A	I	D	W	T	U	R	C	J	O	T
O	H	V	H	C	G	I	C	S	V	K	O	A	U	I	O	K	Q	O	A
U	J	A	X	R	S	M	E	D	C	K	S	N	E	A	F	R	C	E	I
V	O	B	R	M	O	L	F	I	H	A	R	T	S	W	Q	G	O	J	N
E	F	E	U	L	R	F	R	G	V	C	T	T	P	E	Q	U	J	B	C
R	F	U	A	A	E	E	E	A	B	U	G	O	O	R	R	Q	D	U	O
T	F	W	H	X	D	M	G	K	B	U	S	E	T	D	K	I	G	I	L
U	G	C	V	E	K	E	L	M	A	C	F	U	A	N	A	P	E	J	L
R	W	Z	R	C	W	S	A	R	W	F	W	Q	I	O	A	U	Z	S	E
E	U	F	G	V	F	N	D	H	J	G	L	Z	V	S	N	V	Y	L	G
U	V	J	J	V	E	U	S	C	G	C	S	E	A	C	L	O	U	D	E

Find these words

FREDERICKDOUGLASS	HARRIETTUBMAN
BLACKMOUNTAINCOLLEGE	COASTGUARD
HARLEM	CHARLESALSTON
AUGUSTASAVAGE	DYNAMICCUBISM
THEMIGRATIONSERIES	USCGCSEACLOUD
JOHNBROWN	TOUSSAINTLOUVERTURE

79

Directions: Read the text below. Then answer the questions that follow.

A sentence forms a complete thought; it always has a subject and a verb. Give each fragment below a subject and then rewrite the new sentence. **Answers may vary**

1) Works on a ship all day.

2) Assigned the class homework for the weekend.

3) Carefully looked through the paints to find the color green.

4) Cried all day and night without stopping.

5) Wears khaki pants and a tan shirt for his job.

6) Visited a friend on a rainy night.

7) Painted a portrait on the stage.

8) Found a script on the floor and looked really excited.

9) Wears the fanciest dresses in the whole world.

10) Leaves the house and goes to work in Africa.

Directions: Read and answer the questions below. These are the different forms of poetry. There are clues in the puzzle to help you. Try and solve the cryptic message.

Clue for cryptic message: Jacob says this is something a painting should have.

Questions

1) I have a series about the life of _____ Railroad leader Harriet Tubman.

2) I was the first time that a black artist was represented by a _____ gallery.

3) I achieved the rank of petty officer ____ class.

4) In the beginning of my career my style was _____.

5) I attended _____ Alston's classes at the Harlem Art Workshop.

6) My _____ Series was the first artwork by an African-American artist to be purchased by The Museum of Modern Art.

7) Harlem inspired my painting Harlem _____ Scene.

8) I was a professor at the University of _____.

9) I was born in _____ City.

10) I helped represent the United States at the _____ Biennale.

11) I was drafted into the _____ during World War II.

12) _____ is an example of another style I use called Dynamic Cubism.

81

Directions: This is the WGLT Challenge. Solve the cryptogram. As the puzzle solver, you need to find which number belongs to which character. And this can be pretty challenging! You will need to match the number with the letter. There are some letters given to you below. This will help you solve the other words and unlock more characters. **Good Luck.**

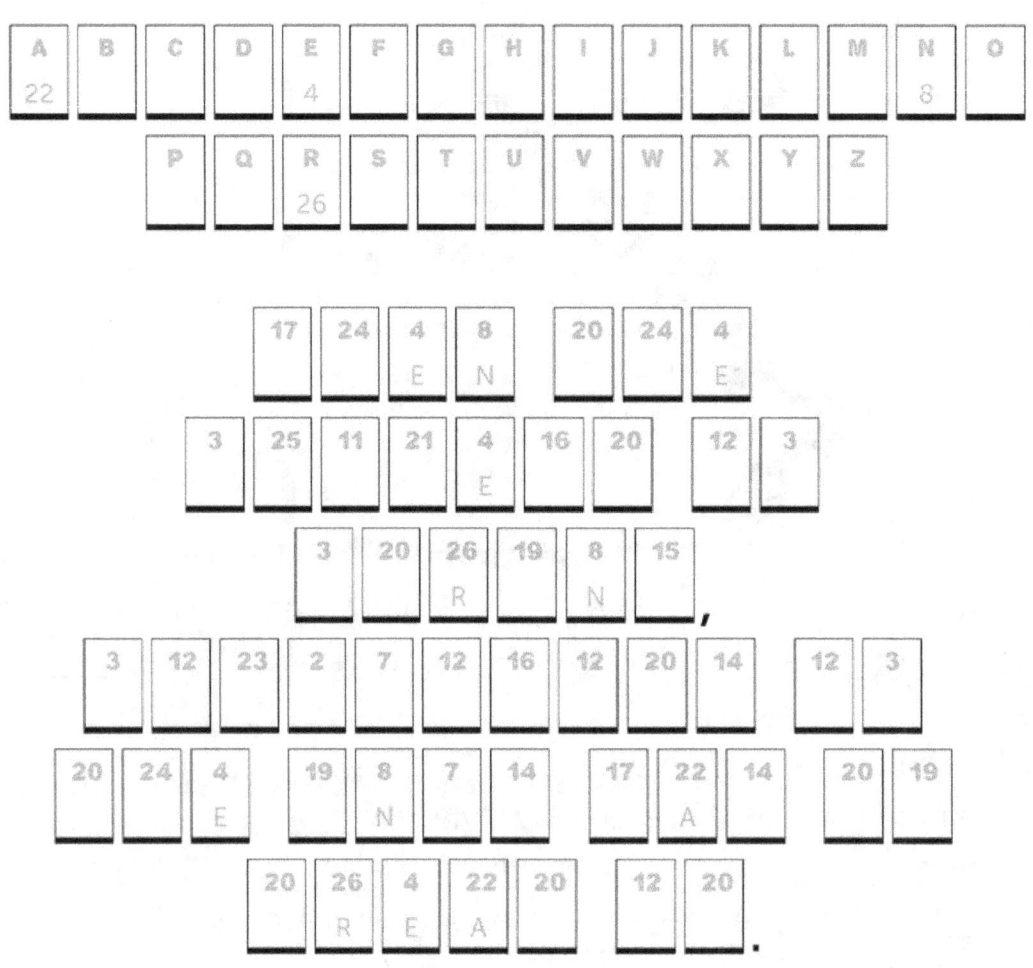

Kara Walker

Kara Walker

November 26, 1969 – Present
PAINTER

83

Kara Walker

Kara Walker

Kara Walker

Kara Walker

Kara Walker

Kara Walker

Hi, my name is Kara Walker. I was born on November 26, 1969, in Stockton, CA. I earned my bachelor's degree from the Atlanta College of Art and my master's degree from the Rhode Island School of Design. I'm known for creating panoramic friezes of cut-paper silhouettes that feature mostly black figures and address the history of American slavery and racism through violent and unsettling imagery. Some of my works of art are Gone, Darkytown Rebellion, Fons Americanus and A Subtlety. I was one of the youngest artists to receive the John D. and Catherine T. MacArthur Foundation Genius Grant at the age of 27. In 2007 I was also listed as one of Time's 100 Most Influential People in the World.

1. What state was I born in?
   A. Florida
   B. Georgia
   C. California
2. What was the name of Magazine I was listed in?
   A. Time
   B. The New Yorker
   C. Ebony
3. Which work of art is not my own?
   A. Pool Parlor
   B. Gone
   C. A Subtlety

Directions: Answer the questions, to solve the crossword puzzle. You can use the internet if you get stuck on any question.

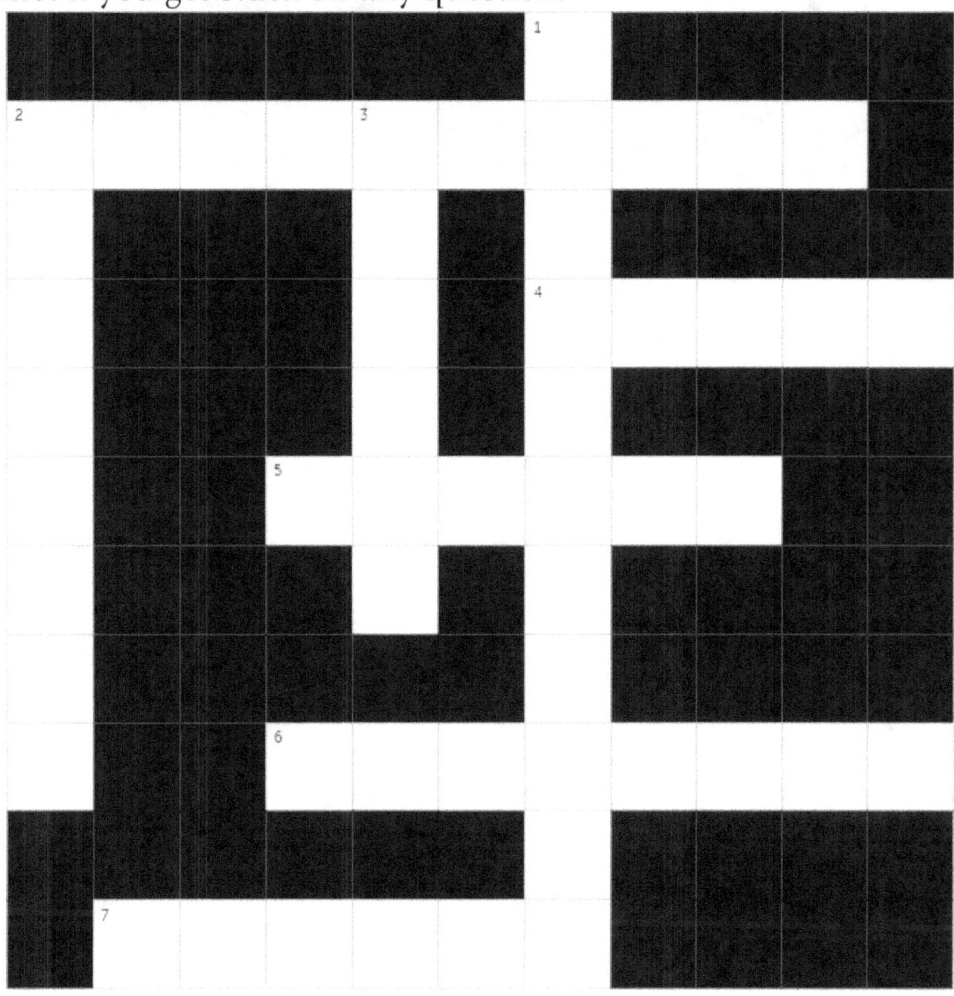

Across

2) When I lived in _____, I was free of any thought of race.

4) Christian ____ had an impact on me and my artwork.

5) I was selected as director, set and costume designer for the production of Vincenzo Bellini's Norma at Teatro La Fenice, _____, Italy.

6) One of my favorite titles of my artwork is the _____.

7) I'm the second youngest recipient of the _____. Grant at 27.

Down

1) I made TIME magazine's most _____ "TIME 100" list.

2) I was a professor of visual arts at _____ University.

3) My ____ inspired me to become an artist.

Directions: Read the text below. Then answer the questions that follow.
A **subject** is what the sentence is about. A **predicate** tells us what the subject is or does. A **sentence** includes both a subject and a predicate.

Decide whether each phrase below is a sentence, a subject, or a predicate. Write your choice.

1.) The black paint. _____

2.) Octavia is tall. _____

3.) Walks to the museum. _____

4.) Lives in Fort Greene. _____

5.) My art, Salvation. _____

6.) We saw the art show. _____

7.) The sister of my uncle. _____

8.) Ate all of the candy. _____

9.) Wants to run a marathon. _____

10.) The nurse helps. _____

11.) Octavia and Dana. _____

12.) Larry loves art. _____

Directions: Unscramble the words below about Kara. See if you can get the bonus word.

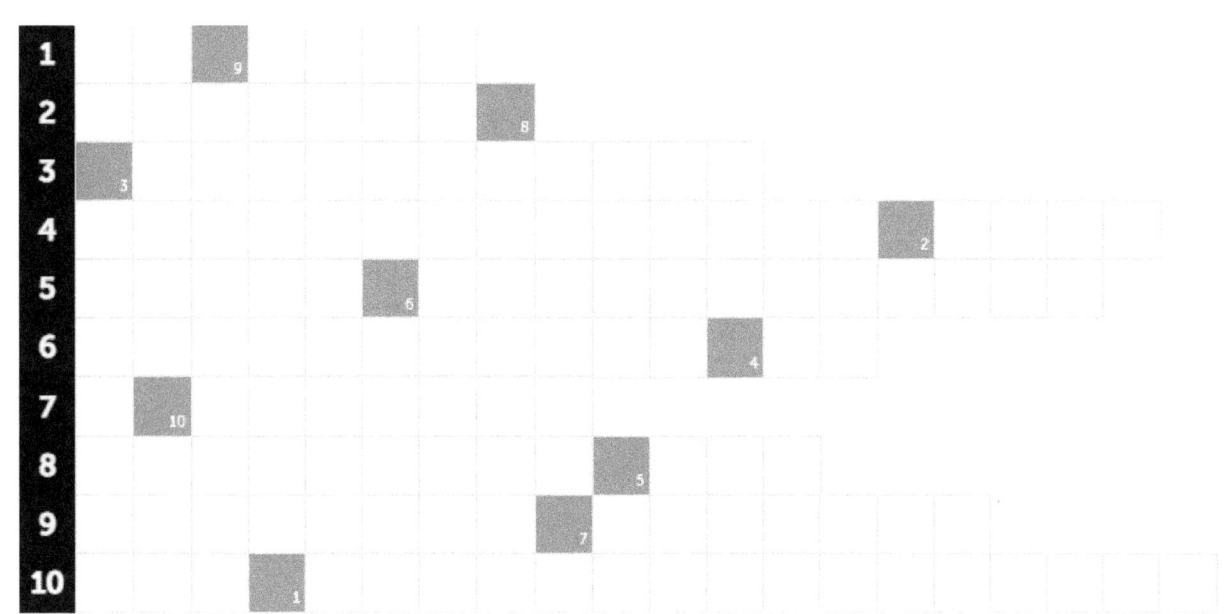

BONUS WORD

1	2	3	4	5	6		7	8	9	10

Unscramble Words

1) eusrgtr
2) kfamiler
3) stutiisehlot
4) epnytpeaorrcmrnaiot
5) stiaaitltniatsorln
6) teleraeghfetud
7) tyseultab
8) moesnnfcauair
9) serenvpatitaoane
10) yhoivnsimntuifcegrai

Directions: This is the WGLT Challenge. Solve the cryptogram. As the puzzle solver, you need to find which number belongs to which character. And this can be pretty challenging! You will need to match the number with the letter. There are some letters given to you below. This will help you solve the other words and unlock more characters. **Good Luck.**

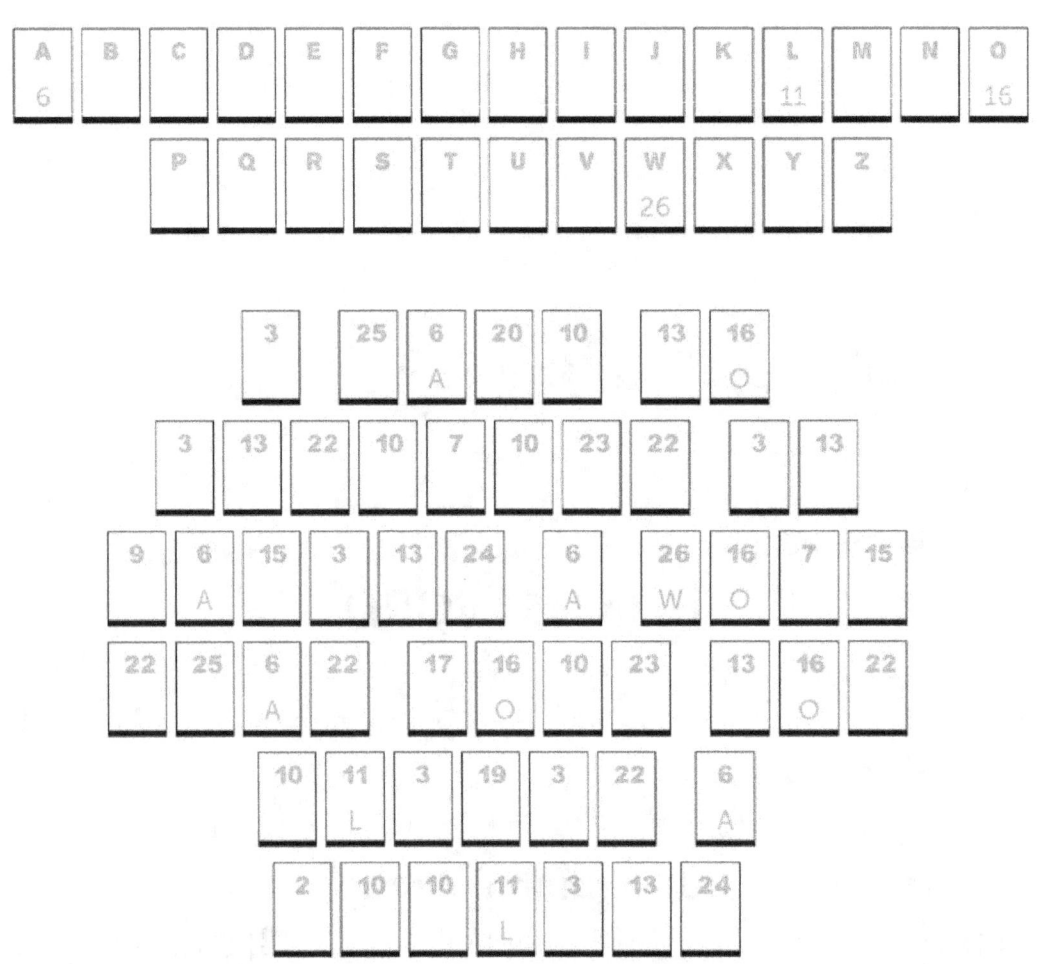

Henry Ossawa Tanner

Henry Ossawa Tanner

June 21, 1859 – May 25, 1937
ARTIST/PAINTER

LEFT BLANK ON PURPOSE

Henry Ossawa Tanner

Henry Ossawa Tanner

Henry Ossawa Tanner

Henry Ossawa Tanner

Henry Ossawa Tanner

Henry Ossawa Tanner

Hi, my name is Henry Tanner. I was born on June 21, 1859, in Pittsburgh, PA. I attended the Pennsylvania Academy of the Fine Arts in Philadelphia. I was the only Black student. I was the first artist to achieve international acclaim. During World War I (WWI), I served with the American Red Cross in France. In 1923, the French government made me a chevalier of the Legion of Honor. In 1927, I became the first African American to be granted full membership in the National Academy of Design in New York. One of the things that I'm best known for is being the first Black artist in the U.S. Some of the works that I'm known for are The Banjo Lesson, The Thankful Poor, Lions in the Desert and The Good Shepherd.

1. In WWI who did I serve with?
   A. Infantry
   B. Red Cross
   C. Cooks
2. I became a member of the National Academy of Design in?
   A. 1920
   B. 1927
   C. 1930
3. What city was my Academy in?
   A. Pittsburgh
   B. Scranton
   C. Philadelphia

Directions: Find the words associated with Henry's life and career.

R	E	A	L	I	S	T	P	A	I	N	T	E	R	W
R	V	E	V	T	T	H	E	A	R	C	H	X	H	V
M	L	M	O	E	F	H	V	W	S	I	Y	I	T	F
C	P	J	P	K	R	Q	C	N	L	G	T	H	H	N
T	M	G	A	Y	L	Y	X	S	A	E	O	L	I	N
M	A	N	H	B	G	H	C	T	H	M	K	I	N	T
V	T	D	I	J	Y	N	E	O	A	C	N	W	S	I
E	S	R	C	U	N	W	U	S	L	S	B	G	M	U
Z	E	V	O	S	A	S	E	R	I	L	F	W	J	G
D	G	B	O	Y	E	A	C	R	N	V	E	H	W	D
E	A	M	K	K	K	L	A	L	M	Q	X	G	Z	I
J	T	R	C	I	M	P	Q	J	C	A	V	N	E	F
C	S	A	N	N	R	G	Z	I	H	S	R	Y	N	P
Q	O	S	B	E	D	Y	K	X	G	Y	A	H	X	K
G	P	R	E	D	C	R	O	S	S	T	X	M	M	X

Find these words

WHITEHOUSE	THOMASEAKINS	AVERYCOLLEGE
PARIS	REALISTPAINTER	GATEWAY
REDCROSS	THEARCH	POSTAGESTAMP

Have you ever wanted to design something? If so what was it, if not what would you do instead.

Whats your favorite tyoes of movies to go to?

What goals do you have for yourself? What are 5 things you want to do before you are (21)?

Directions: Read and answer the questions below. These are the different forms of poetry. There are clues in the puzzle to help you. Try and solve the cryptic message.

Clue for cryptic message: This is one of Henry's paintings he created.

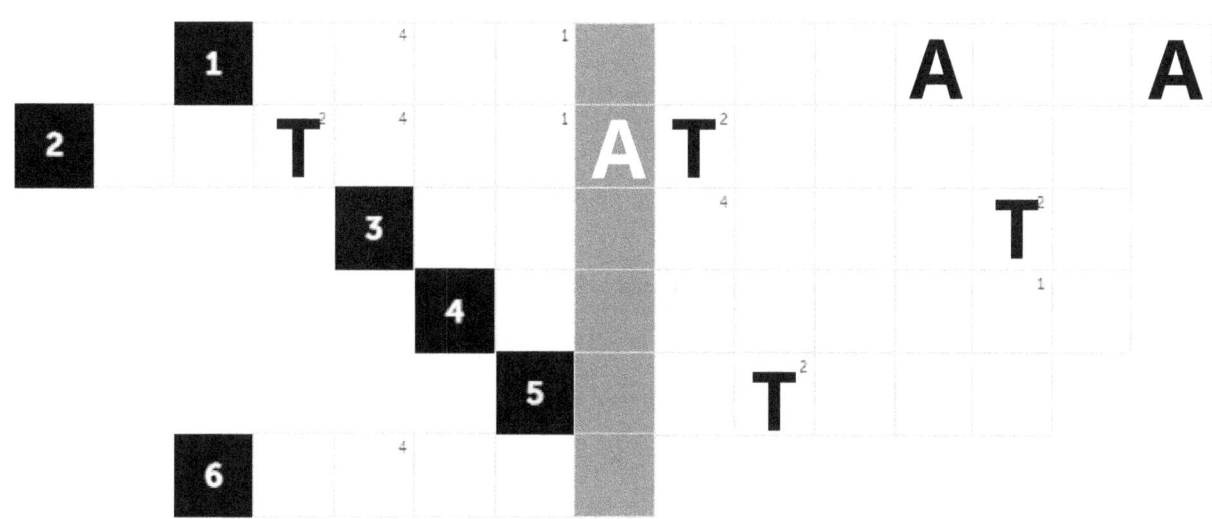

Questions

1) I trained at the _____ Academy of Fine Arts.

2) I was the first artist of his race to achieve _____ acclaim.

3) I'm considered to be the first African American _____ artist

4) I'm regarded as a realist painter, _____ on accurate depictions of subjects.

5) _____ of Henry O. Tanner is displayed in the Smithsonian American Art Museum.

6) The Banjo Lesson painting is considered _____ art.

Directions: This is the WGLT Challenge. Solve the cryptogram. As the puzzle solver, you need to find which number belongs to which character. And this can be pretty challenging! You will need to match the number with the letter. There are some letters given to you below. This will help you solve the other words and unlock more characters. **Good Luck.**

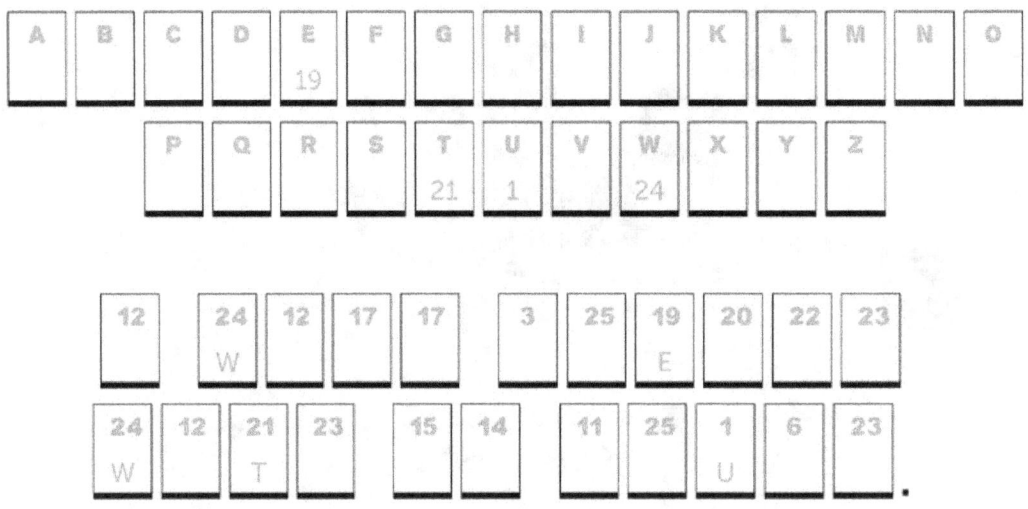

Edmonia Lewis

Edmonia Lewis

July 4, 1844 – September 17, 1907

SCULPTOR

LEFT BLANK ON PURPOSE

Edmonia Lewis

Edmonia Lewis

Edmonia Lewis

Edmonia Lewis

Edmonia Lewis

Edmonia Lewis

Hi, my name is Mary Edmonia Lewis. I was born on July 4, 1844, in Albany, NY. I also went by "Wildfire," which was my Native American name. I attended the New York Central College, as well as Oberlin College in Ohio. I was the first African American and Native American sculptor to achieve national and international prominence. One of the things that I'm best known for is participating in the 1876 Centennial Exposition in Philadelphia, where I sculpted The Death of Cleopatra. Some of my sculptures are Forever Free, Hagar and Old Arrow-Maker and His Daughter. I was often inspired by the lives of abolitionists and Civil War heroes.

1. What college didn't I go to?
   A. Oberlin College
   B. Michigan University
   C. New York Central College
2. What year did I participate in Centennial Exposition?
   A. 1920
   B. 1876
   C. 1870
3. What is one of my inspiration?
   A. WW I heroes
   B. WW II heroes
   C. Abolitionists

Directions: Answer the questions, to solve the crossword puzzle. You can use the internet if you get stuck on any question.

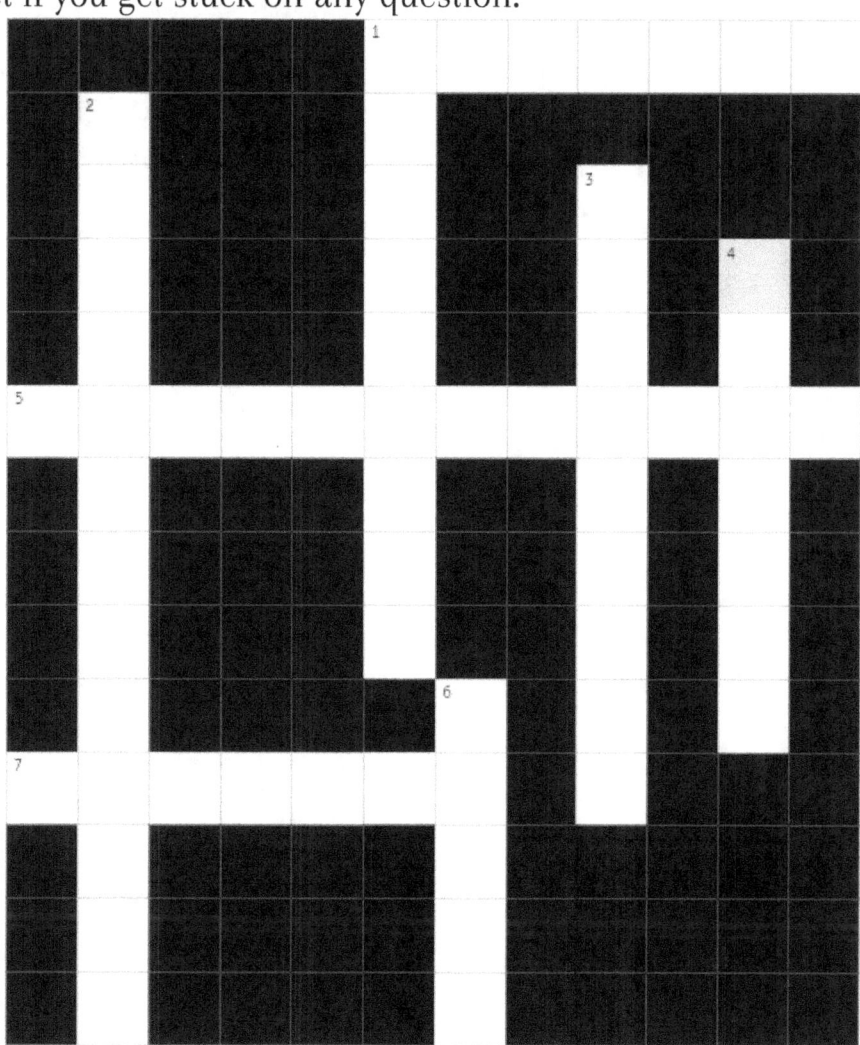

Across

1) I attended _____ College which was one of the first institutions of higher education to admit African Americans.

5) I'm considered the first _____ BIPOC sculptor in the United States

7) Some say my sculpture _____ Free is my best work.

Down

1) Some of my sculptures where about _____ black people.

2) I was the first sculptor of African American and Native American descent to achieve _____ recognition.

3) In 1876, I presented my work The Death of _____ at the Philadelphia Centennial Exposition.

4) I started to work with_____ when I moved to Rome.

6) U.S. President _____ commissioned me to do his portrait.

Directions: Read the text below. Then answer the questions that follow.

Match each term with its definition.

A) chisels   B) respirator   C) Safety glasses
D) work bench   E) lift   F) ear plugs
G) gloves   H) rasps   I) sandpaper
J) Marble   K) Clay   L) Stone

_____ A coarse file or similar metal tool with a roughened surface for filing, down hard materials.

_____ A long-bladed hand tool with a beveled cutting edge.

_____ Paper with sand or another abrasive stuck to it.

_____ An apparatus worn over the mouth and nose or the entire face to prevent the inhalation of dust.

_____ A covering for the hand worn for protection against cold or dirt.

_____ A flat table or surface at which practical work is done.

_____ A piece of wax, rubber, or cotton placed in the ear as protection against noise or water.

_____ A device incorporating a moving cable for carrying things or people.

Directions: Unscramble the words below about Edmonia. See if you can get the bonus word.

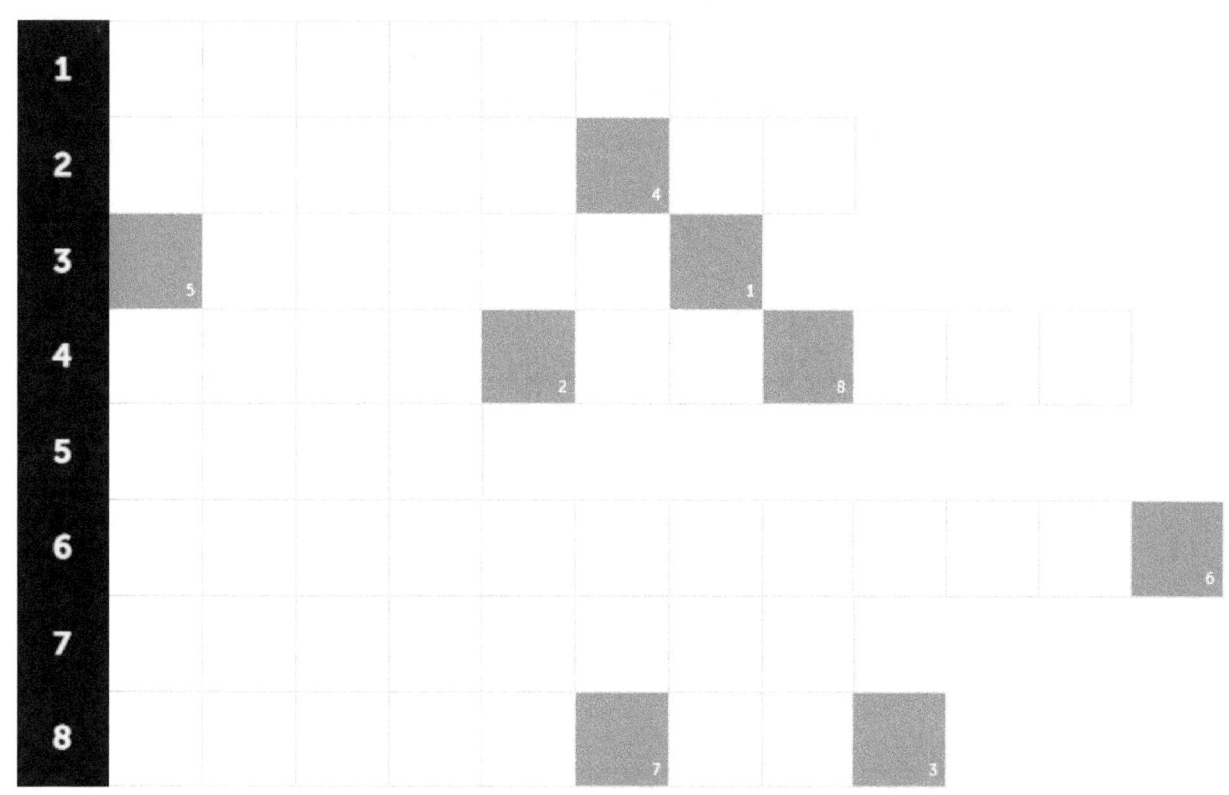

BONUS WORD

1	2	3	4	5	6	7	8

Unscramble Words

1) Lnonod

2) icwilvra

3) lahbsoi

4) iasuMssaisg

5) meRo

6) ittioolasinb

7) lrscuotp

8) Mnaanhhei

Directions: This is the WGLT Challenge. Solve the cryptogram. As the puzzle solver, you need to find which number belongs to which character. And this can be pretty challenging! You will need to match the number with the letter. There are some letters given to you below. This will help you solve the other words and unlock more characters. **Good Luck.**

A	B	C	D	E	F	G	H	I	J	K	L	M	N	O
23							17	1						

P	Q	R	S	T	U	V	W	X	Y	Z
							14			

1	5	17	26	3	6	17	5		1		4	18	8	14
I		H				H			I					W

8	15	8	19	21	5	17	1	18	6		14	17	8	18
						H	I				W	H		

1	10	23	16	8		5	26		19	26	16	8
I		A										|,

24	3	5	1		9	26	26	18	2	26	3	18	7
			I										

1	17	23	7
I	H	A	

8	15	8	19	21	5	17	1	18	6		5	26
						H	I					

22	8	23	19	18
		A		|.

Langston Hughes

Langston Hughes

February 1, 1901 – May 22, 1967
POET

107

LEFT BLANK ON PURPOSE

Langston Hughes

Langston Hughes

Langston Hughes

Langston Hughes

Langston Hughes

Langston Hughes

Hi, my name is James Langston Hughes. I was born on February 1, 1901, in Joplin, MO. I attended Central High School in Cleveland, OH. I wrote for the school newspaper and edited the yearbook. I went to Lincoln University in Pennsylvania. I joined Omega Psi Phi and earned my bachelor's degree. One of the things that I'm best known for is my jazz poetry. Some of the works I'm known for include "The Weary Blues," "One-Way Ticket," Famous American Negroes and "Mulatto." I was a reporter for the Chicago Defender, which was an influential African American newspaper. One of my first poems was "The Negro Speaks of Rivers," which I dedicated to W.E.B. DuBois in 1921. I also helped bring light to the Harlem Renaissance movement.

1. What am I know for?
   A. Movies
   B. Jazz Poetry
   C. Children Books
2. What is the name of my fraternity?
   A. Alpha Phi Alpha
   B. Omega Psi Phi
   C. Kappa Alpha Psi
3. What city was I born in?
   A. Chicago
   B. Joplin
   C. Philadelphia

Directions: Find the words associated with Langston's life and career.

```
N  J  C  H  I  C  A  G  O  D  E  F  E  N  D  E  R  M
T  O  S  M  U  L  A  T  T  O  W  L  T  L  N  Q  F  Y
C  Q  T  O  E  A  A  E  J  S  Z  U  U  S  V  X  K  P
B  A  C  W  C  A  C  V  Y  C  K  D  P  F  G  W  M  N
X  W  R  Z  I  I  E  S  B  R  Y  A  V  F  Z  L  F  J
H  E  Z  T  T  A  Y  T  U  C  S  Z  B  G  S  G
D  Y  Z  Y  E  X  H  L  B  B  O  E  T  X  W  N  U  Q
P  H  Y  S  U  R  D  O  A  J  G  H  O  V  Q  K  G  L
Y  Y  J  I  Z  G  G  Y  U  C  W  A  I  P  L  H  V  I
I  I  J  S  H  E  M  W  X  T  T  D  K  V  Z  L  N  T
X  O  N  I  G  R  J  T  O  L  L  I  J  Q  S  Z  R  Z
C  G  P  R  E  Q  T  Z  V  O  I  A  V  T  B  B  A  W
T  L  O  C  C  X  F  J  Z  Q  D  J  U  I  D  U  T  J
B  S  E  E  I  H  Q  C  Z  U  Y  S  K  G  S  C  I  Q
J  M  T  H  P  J  F  D  Z  F  Q  X  O  F  H  T  I  G
Z  Z  V  T  C  D  H  Q  G  V  Y  A  Y  N  E  T  A  U
H  A  R  L  E  M  R  E  N  A  I  S  S  A  N  C  E  C
L  I  N  C  O  L  N  U  N  I  V  E  R  S  I  T  Y  R
```

Find These Words

NOTWITHOUTLAUGHTER   SOCIALACTIVIST

HARLEMRENAISSANCE   THECRISIS

JAZZPOETRY   CARTERGWOODSON

POET   CHICAGODEFENDER

MULATTO   LINCOLNUNIVERSITY

111

Directions: Read the text below. Then answer the questions that follow.

Let's learn about continents. A **continent** is one of Earth's seven main divisions of land. The continents are, from largest to smallest: **Asia**, **Africa**, **North America**, **South America**, **Antarctica, Europe**, and **Australia**. Langston was able to visit four continents while he was alive. **Here are some of the places. Lets see if you can match it to the right continent. Draw a line to the correct continent. A continent may have more than one answer.**

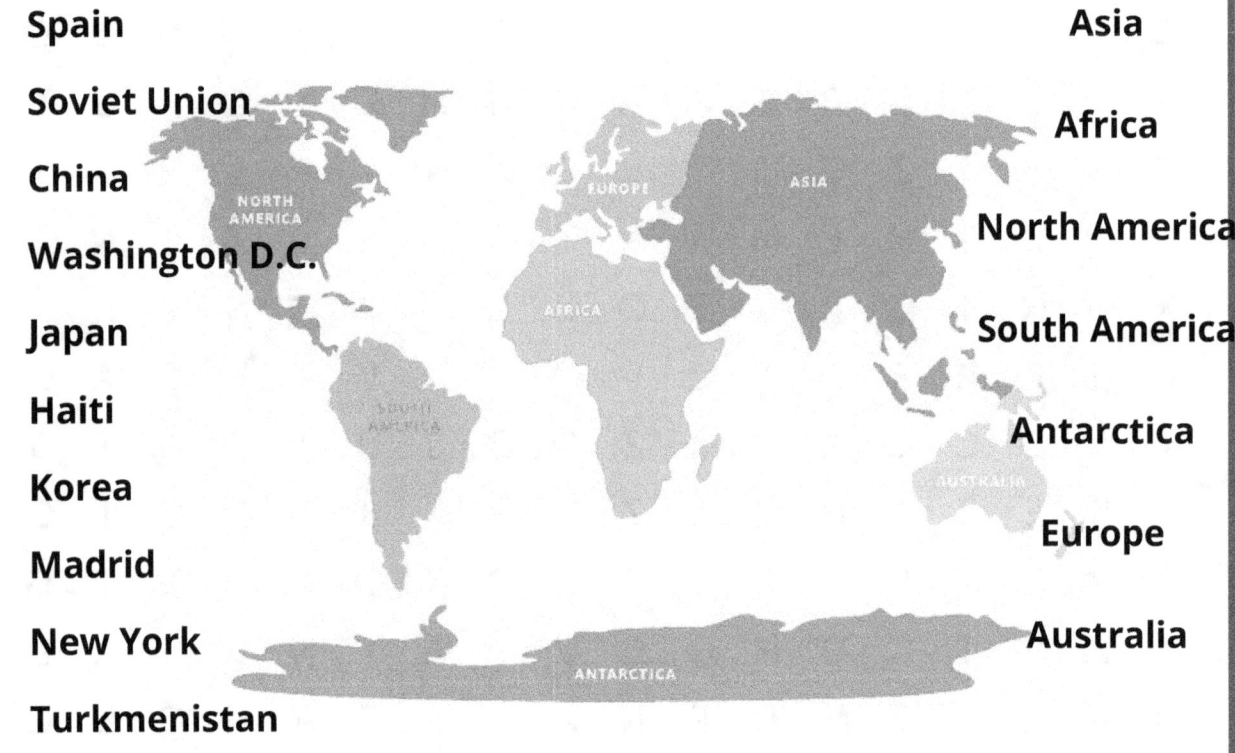

Spain	**Asia**
Soviet Union	**Africa**
China	**North America**
Washington D.C.	**South America**
Japan	**Antarctica**
Haiti	**Europe**
Korea	**Australia**
Madrid	
New York	
Turkmenistan	

1) What continent do you live on?

2) What city or town do you live in?

3) How many people live in your city or town?

4) Name three countries and cities or towns you would love to visit?

112

Directions: Read and answer the questions below. These are the different forms of poetry. There are clues in the puzzle to help you. Try and solve the cryptic message.

Clue for cryptic message: This is one of Langston's' famous jazz poems.

Questions

1) Some say I'm the _____ of jazz poetry.

2) I went to the Soviet Union to make a film called Black and ____ but we never finished it.

3) At 17 I wrote one of my most famous poetry works, "The ____ Speaks of Rivers"

4) I was able to help Carter G. Woodson catalog new and _____ experiences and achievements of African Americans.

5) Me and Richard Nugent launched the magazine ____.

6) During my life I never _____ or had children.

7) The new Fresh Prince of Bel-Air reboot used my poem _____ to Son in one of there trailers.

8) The Black _____ often called me The People's Poet.

9) I had a lot of activists and _____ in my family.

10) During my life I have been able to _____ the world.

11) I studied Engineering while at _____ University.

12) I worked for the Chicago _____ for twenty years.

13) In 1937, I worked for The Baltimore Afro-American newspaper and reported on the _____ Civil War.

113

Directions: This is the WGLT Challenge. Solve the cryptogram. As the puzzle solver, you need to find which number belongs to which character. And this can be pretty challenging! You will need to match the number with the letter. There are some letters given to you below. This will help you solve the other words and unlock more characters. **Good Luck.**

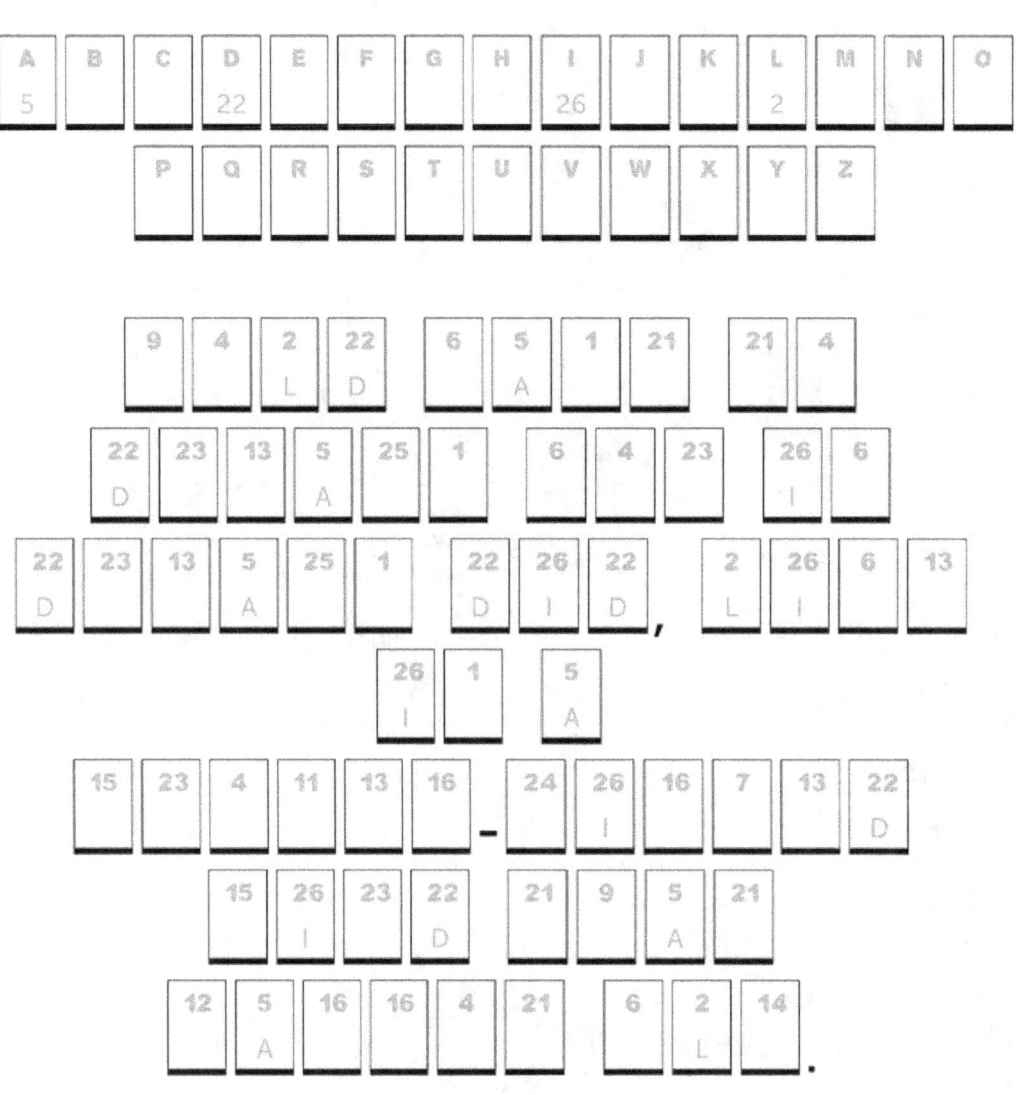

A	B	C	D	E	F	G	H	I	J	K	L	M	N	O
5			22					26			2			

P	Q	R	S	T	U	V	W	X	Y	Z

Maya Angelou

Maya Angelou

April 4, 1928 – May 28, 2014
WRITER/POET

LEFT BLANK ON PURPOSE

Maya Angelou

Maya Angelou

Maya Angelou

Maya Angelou

Maya Angelou

Maya Angelou

Hi, my name is Maya Angelou. I was born on April 4, 1928, in St. Louis, MO. I attended the California Labor School in San Francisco, CA. When I was a teenager, I got what I felt was my dream job, which was being a streetcar conductor in San Francisco. I was the first Black woman to be hired for that position. One of the things that I'm best known for is my unique autobiographical writing style. Some of the works that I'm known for are I Know Why the Caged Bird Sings, The Heart of a Woman, A Song Flung Up to Heaven and Mom & Me & Mom. I also wrote Hallmark greeting cards. I was the first Black poet to present at a presidential inauguration. The poem that I presented was called "On the Pulse of Morning," which I won a Grammy for.

1. What was my dream job as a teen?
   A. Cook
   B. Streetcar Conductor
   C. Poet
2. What poem did I win a Grammy for?
   A. Still I Rise
   B. On The Pulse of Morning
   C. The Heart of a Woman
3. What city did I attend school?
   A. Pittsburgh
   B. San Francisco
   C. New York

Directions: Answer the questions, to solve the crossword puzzle. You can use the internet if you get stuck on any question.

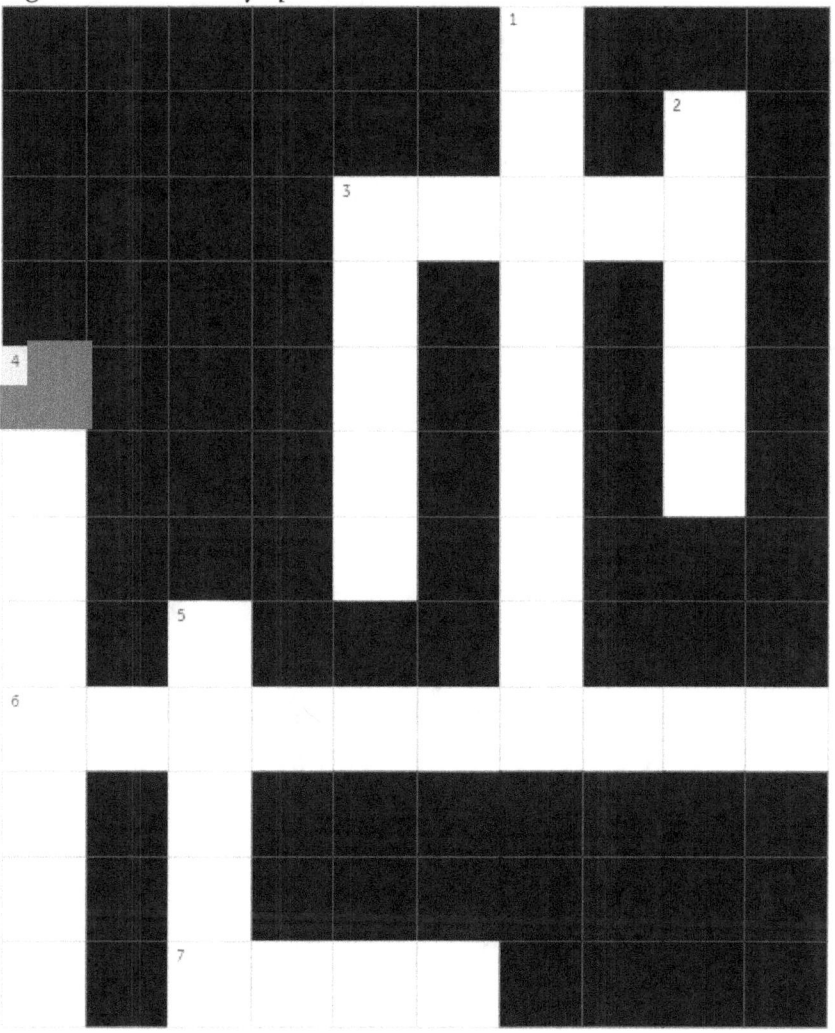

Across

3) I worked for a newspaper in ___, Egypt.

6) I was a coordinator for the Southern Christian _____ Conference, a black civil rights organization.

7) I was the Director for the film _____ in the Delta.

Down

1) I wrote "On the Pulse of Morning" for President _____ inauguration.

2) I was a cast member of the opera Porgy and Bess.

3) I WAS THE FIRST BLACK WOMAN TO CONDUCT A ____ CAR IN SAN FRANCISCO.

4) I spoke six languages English, French, Spanish, Hebrew, _____ and Fante (a dialect of Akan native to Ghana).

5) My first book I Know Why the ____ Bird Sings was a best seller.

Directions: Read the Poem below. Then answer the questions that follow.

My beautiful black queens

Yo don't believe the hype
everything they told you
it wasn't right

Your black your ugly a woman
your nothing
Well I'm here to tell you
that your something

Clever innovative and beautiful
From your toe nails
up to your cuticles

Don't let anyone taint your worth
Continue to stay strong
until that ride in a hearse

1) What are the three words used to describe Black Queens.

2) What shouldn't you believe in the poem.

3) What do you think the word taint means in the poem.

4) What is something people have said about Black women in the poem.

Directions: Unscramble the words below about Maya. See if you can get the bonus word.

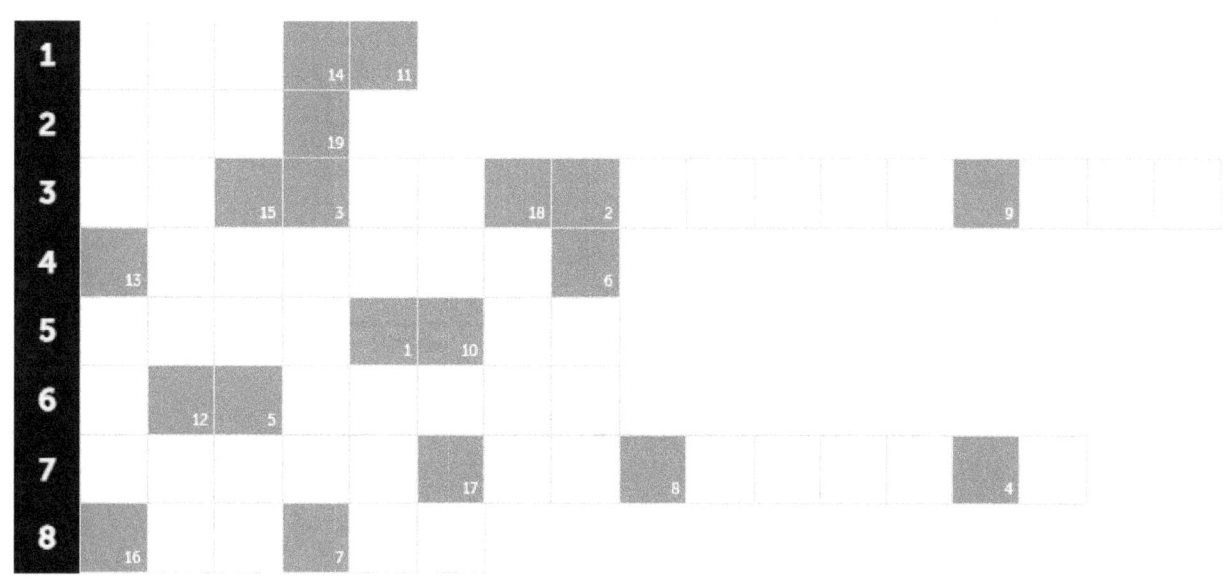

BONUS WORD

1	2	3	4	5	6	7	8	9	10	11	12	13	14	15	16	17	18	19

Unscramble Words

1) orsot

2) etpo

3) fvigyeuornitahsna

4) mopocers

5) cterdior

6) cmxamoll

7) aarrgegoggieio,

8) niceve

Directions: This is the WGLT Challenge. Solve the cryptogram. As the puzzle solver, you need to find which number belongs to which character. And this can be pretty challenging! You will need to match the number with the letter. There are some letters given to you below. This will help you solve the other words and unlock more characters. **Good Luck.**

Etheridge Knight

Etheridge Knight

123

April 19, 1931 – March 10, 1991
POET

LEFT BLANK ON PURPOSE

Etheridge Knight

Etheridge Knight

Etheridge Knight

Etheridge Knight

Etheridge Knight

Etheridge Knight

Hi, my name is Etheridge Knight. I was born on April 9, 1931, in Corinth, MS. In 1947, I enlisted in the Army and served as a medical technician in the Korean War until 1950. I was hit by shrapnel and sustained serious injuries, as well as psychological trauma, because of this incident. I turned to morphine to take the pain away. A few years later, I was arrested for armed robbery and ended up being sent to prison for eight years. During this time is when I started writing poetry. One of the things I'm best known for is Poems from Prison. Gwendolyn Brooks, Dudley Randall and Sonia Sanchez came to visit me. Later, Dudley published Poems from Prison in the Broadside Press and hailed me as one of the major poets of the Black Arts Movement.

1. What year did I enlist in the Army?
   A. 1950
   B. 1947
   C. 1948
2. What did I go to prison for?
   A. selling drugs
   B. assault
   C. armed robbery
3. What poet didn't visit me in prison?
   A. Langston Hughes
   B. Sonia Sanchez
   C. Gwendolyn Brooks

Directions: Find the words associated with Etheridge's life and career.

```
R Q X G S J K P O E T R Y B L J Q C
G I H U S K L O U Z O B X W H H F T
B L A C K A R T S M O V E M E N T B
I E G R Q A A T I F F V O W I R R N
T O D I N A H W A S H I N G T O N I
G V B M J R C H B Z J V Q U I Y F B
C A D I J D B A D H O H H V E N U V
W E H N Z D M B B W B A Y B N L T N
S R I A O B H K K Q Q I Z E A V W T
O O Z L W S Q I F W W K V R K D P U
C K T J V A I H H D M U M W P Y R P
Y P M U J L E R J V O Y Q M Y M Z X
A R G S R R E N P A C U A V Q Y Y Q
H A R T F O R D U N I V E R S I T Y
E L G I D D O O W X Z M I P V X Z Y
I T J C U E J O B V G P V K Y G D I
Y F S E Q J F X D Q Q J O Q I K Q G
N E G R O D I G E S T M V A E V X W
```

Find These Words

PRISON

POETRY

BLACKARTSMOVEMENT

ARMY

KOREA

TODINAHWASHINGTON

HARTFORDUNIVERSITY

CRIMINALJUSTICE

NEGRODIGEST

HAIKU

Directions: Read the text below. Then answer the questions that follow.

Circle the word that correctly completes each sentence.

1) Etheridge Knight attain recognition as a major poet, (**earn, earning, earned**) both Pulitzer Prize and National Book Award.

2) Me and my wife Sonia Sanchez were important (**member, members, membered**) of the poets and artists connected to the Black Arts Movement.

3) I joined the Army at the age of eighteen, (**serves, serving, served**) as a medical technician.

4) My first poem, "To Dinah Washington," was (**publish, publishing, published**) in Negro Digest.

5) I (**earn, earned, earning**) a bachelor's degree in American poetry and criminal justice from Martin Center University

6) Etheridge Knight was (**wounds, wounded, wounding**) by shrapnel while serving in the Korea War.

Directions: Read and answer the questions below. These are the different forms of poetry. There are clues in the puzzle to help you. Try and solve the cryptic message.

Clue for cryptic message: Etheridge received this at one time in his career.

Questions

1) My debut work was called Poems from _____.

2) Some of my poems I used _____ in them.

3) I was the writer-in-residence at the _____ University.

4) I started by sending my poems to Negro Digest in 1965.

5) I was considered one of the major poets of the Black Art _____.

6) My wife Sonia _____ was a poet too.

7) I used Black _____ in some of my poems.

8) While I was in the U.S. Army I was stationed in _____.

Directions: This is the WGLT Challenge. Solve the cryptogram. As the puzzle solver, you need to find which number belongs to which character. And this can be pretty challenging! You will need to match the number with the letter. There are some letters given to you below. This will help you solve the other words and unlock more characters. **Good Luck.**

Margaret Walker

Margaret Walker

July 7, 1915 – November 30, 1998
WRITER/POET

131

LEFT BLANK ON PURPOSE

Margaret Walker

Margaret Walker

Margaret Walker

Margaret Walker

Margaret Walker

Margaret Walker

Hi, my name is Margaret Walker. I was born on July 7, 1915, in Birmingham, AL. I received my Bachelor of Arts degree from Northwestern University and my master's in creative writing and Ph.D. from the University of Iowa. I was a literature professor at Jackson State University and founded the Institute for the Study of History, Life and Culture of Black People in 1968. Some of the works that I'm known for are For My People, the novel Jubilee, This Is My Century: New and Collected Poems and October Journey. I began my work in 1936 with the Federal Writers' Project under the Works Progress Administration of President Franklin D. Roosevelt during the Great Depression. I was inducted into The Chicago Literary Hall of Fame in 2014.

1. What is my highest level of education?
   A. Bachelors Degree
   B. Ph.D.
   C. Masters Degree
2. What University did I teach at?
   A. University of Iowa
   B. Jackson State University
   C. Northwestern University
3. What year did I get inducted into The Chicago Literary HOF?
   A. 1998
   B. 2000
   C. 2014

Directions: Answer the questions, to solve the crossword puzzle. You can use the internet if you get stuck on any question.

Across

2) I worked for the Federal _____ Project in Chicago.

6) I got my Bachelor of Arts degree from _____ University.

7) I was a literature professor at _____ State University.

8) _____ is the story of a slave family during and after the Civil War and is based on her great-grandmother's life.

Down

1) Margaret Walker founded the Institute for the Study of History, Life and _____ of Black People.

3) I was part of the African-American literary movement known as the Chicago Black _____.

4) The novel Jubilee was translated into ____ languages and went through 43 printings.

5) For My People won the Yale Series of _____ Poets Competition.

Directions: Read the text below. Then answer the questions that follow.

Rewrite the sentences below with the correct capitalization.

Capitalize the first word in a sentence, proper names of people, places and products, main words in titles and days, months and holidays.

1) my favorite book is "jubilee".

2) for christmas, we listen to "jingle bells" and dress like elves.

3) on friday, my mom is taking me shopping in illinois for new nike shoes.

4) my grandma visits orland in june.

5) we read "for my people" by margaret walker last august.

6) on tuesday, president kennedy will be honored in washington, d. c.

7) i learned about president obama in a book called "a promised land".

8) for memorial day, we visit my grandpa in mississippi.

Directions: Unscramble the words below about Margaret. See if you can get the bonus word.

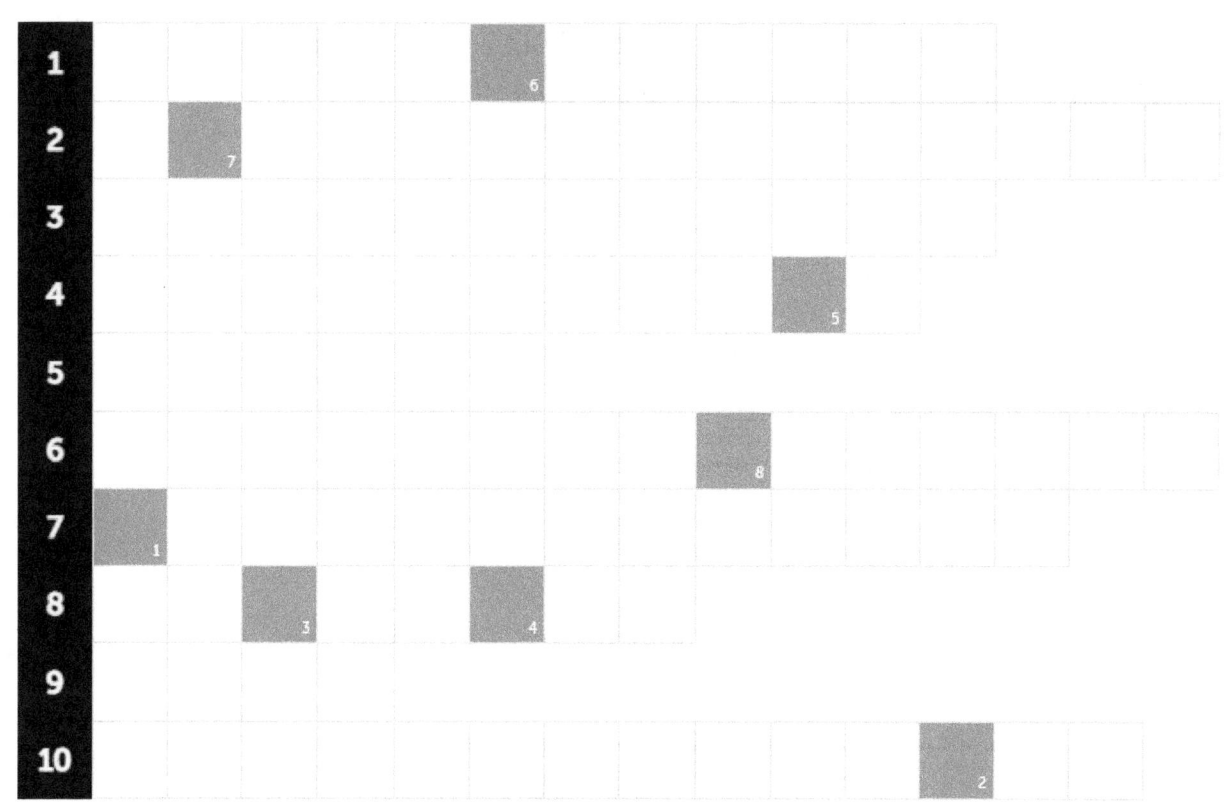

BONUS WORD

1	2	3	4	5	6	7	8

Unscramble Words

1) owtneertshnr   2) uarggntgarsdame   3) ssatokajntce

4) plyeropfmeo   5) rrtiew   6) lrkcsfwoyeordsa

7) anaecdcandwar   8) tlvienos   9) etop

10) npeaziyreamtgo

Directions: This is the WGLT Challenge. Solve the cryptogram. As the puzzle solver, you need to find which number belongs to which character. And this can be pretty challenging! You will need to match the number with the letter. There are some letters given to you below. This will help you solve the other words and unlock more characters. **Good Luck.**

A	B	C	D	E	F	G	H	I	J	K	L	M	N	O
7											17			22

P	Q	R	S	T	U	V	W	X	Y	Z
		23								

Row 1: 10, 23 (R), 20, 16, 4, 13, 9, | 7 (A), 4, 13

Row 2: 1, 22 (O), 22 (O), 13, | 5, 7 (A), 4, 4, 16, 23 (R), 9

Row 3: 19, 20, 17 (L), 17 (L), | 6, 7 (A), 23 (R), 23 (R), 11, | 11, 22 (O), 3

Row 4: 19, 26, 16, 23 (R), 16, | 5, 22 (O), 4, 16, 11

Row 5: 19, 22 (O), 4, 18, | 1, 22 (O).

138

Jean-Michel Basquiat

Jean-Michel Basquiat

December 22, 1960 – August 12, 1988

ARTIST

139

Jean-Michel Basquiat

Jean-Michel Basquiat

Jean-Michel Basquiat

Jean-Michel Basquiat

Jean-Michel Basquiat

Jean-Michel Basquiat

Hi, my name is Jean-Michel Basquiat. I was born on December 22, 1960, in Park Slope, Brooklyn, NY. I attended City-As-School in NY. While there, I made friends with a schoolmate, Al Diaz and we created the pseudonym "SAMO." We began spray-painting graffiti on buildings in Lower Manhattan. We used poetic and satirical advertising slogans in our graffiti. I sold my first painting to Debbie Harry from the band Blondie. I also appeared in her video "Rapture" as the DJ. One of the things I'm best known for is an art exhibition. After I became a junior member of the Brooklyn Museum, they hosted One Basquiat, which was an exhibition that was devoted solely to me. I set a record for having one of my pieces sell for the highest-ever price at auction. The price paid for my piece was $110.5 million.

1. What was my pseudonym name?
   A. Milo
   B. SAMO
   C. Skana
2. What was the video I appeared in?
   A. Fight the power
   B. Rapture
   C. Rock the bells
3. What museum hosted my exhibition?
   A. Metropolitan Museum of Art
   B. Brooklyn Museum
   C. The Frick

Directions: Find the words associated with Jean Michel's life and career.

A	P	C	Y	H	I	E	S	O	N	A	N	I	N	N	A	E	U
D	J	U	R	S	Z	G	V	X	G	T	P	X	W	S	O	Q	N
N	E	O	-	E	X	P	R	E	S	S	I	O	N	I	S	M	S
N	U	B	N	K	Y	Y	E	D	Q	M	T	H	F	I	M	R	N
E	K	1	B	X	C	L	A	P	E	A	I	N	F	Y	D	E	A
T	Z	8	L	I	A	P	U	J	E	L	Y	O	B	A	R	B	V
Y	E	N	N	N	E	C	P	E	J	K	T	S	V	M	X	O	B
Y	Y	W	K	V	I	H	L	D	I	V	E	I	A	Y	L	A	E
V	O	O	F	Z	X	G	A	C	V	H	E	J	T	V	T	F	A
T	M	T	A	Y	A	X	Q	R	C	C	G	W	C	N	R	R	T
T	A	N	H	P	O	F	D	I	R	J	Q	T	E	A	U	T	B
W	S	W	J	Y	X	W	R	R	Z	Y	E	M	P	Y	R	A	O
D	J	O	N	D	U	O	R	M	H	I	U	T	Y	N	A	L	P
F	W	D	C	Y	T	M	Y	X	F	C	U	I	R	Q	B	B	X
G	M	R	Q	E	P	N	I	P	O	R	X	V	E	Y	O	I	Z
Q	I	D	G	G	H	Y	A	D	E	I	Y	L	A	D	X	B	R
M	J	A	S	O	A	C	V	K	L	X	Y	Y	R	A	J	T	C
L	R	G	E	D	O	H	C	G	H	S	B	E	H	K	J	R	W

Find These Words

DEBBIEHARRY   RAGETORICHES   UNTITLED

BEATBOP   SAMO   RAPTURE

DOCUMENTA   DOWNTOWN81   NEO-EXPRESSIONISM

ANNINANOSEI

Directions: This is an Internet search assignment. Read and answer the questions below.
Look up the following paintings by Jean-Michel Basquiat. Untitled, Crown, Hollywood Africans and La Hara.

1) Which painting is your favorite. _____

2) Why is that your favorite painting. _____

3) In the empty space below draw your interpretation of a Jean-Michel painting.

Directions: Read and answer the questions below. These are the different forms of poetry. There are clues in the puzzle to help you. Try and solve the cryptic message.

Clue for cryptic message: Jean-Michel's made history with this work of art.

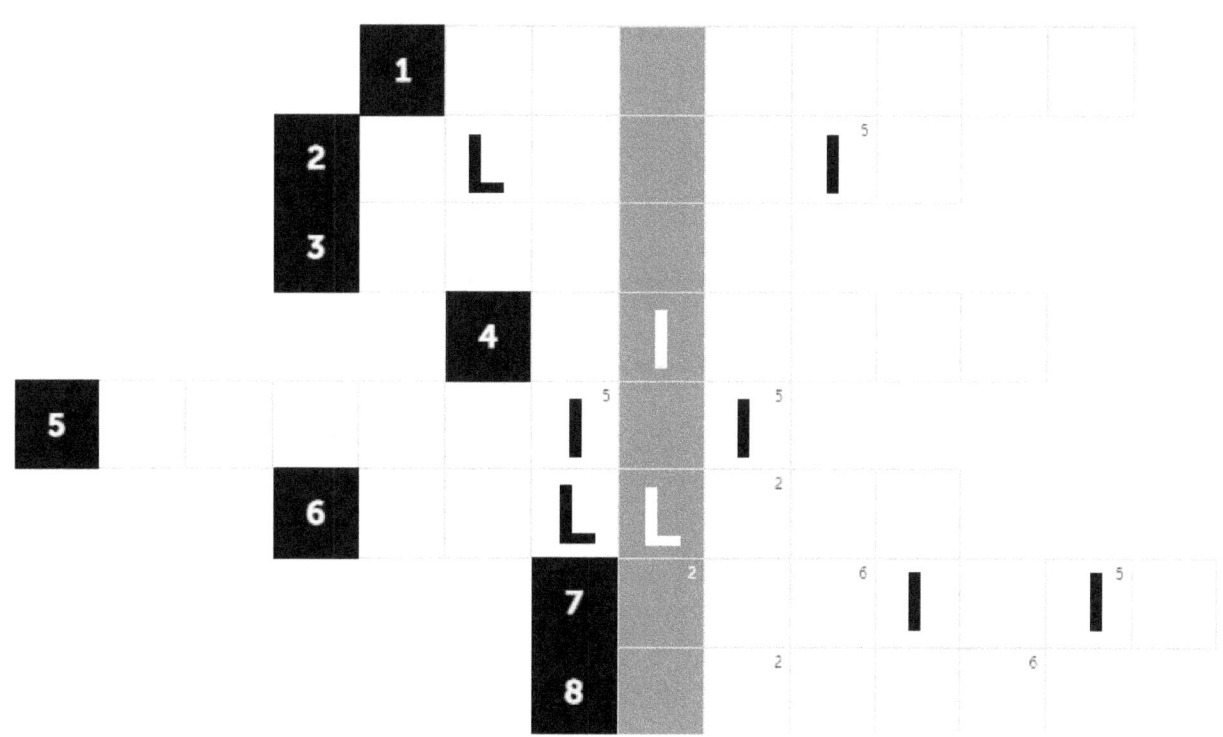

Questions

1) I was the _____ artist to ever take part in Documenta in Kassel.

2) appeared as a disc jockey in the 1981 _____ music video "Rapture".

3) I appeared on the live television program TV ____.

4) Jean-Michel's life documentary is called Basquiat:Rage to ____.

5) I began spray painting ____ on buildings in Lower Manhattan.

6) In November 1982, Basquiat's solo exhibition opened at the Fun _____ in the East Village.

7) At 22, Jean-Michel was one of the youngest to _____ at the Whitney Biennial in New York.

8) One of Basquiat's final paintings was Riding with _____.

Directions: This is the WGLT Challenge. Solve the cryptogram. As the puzzle solver, you need to find which number belongs to which character. And this can be pretty challenging! You will need to match the number with the letter. There are some letters given to you below. This will help you solve the other words and unlock more characters. **Good Luck.**

June Jordan

June Jordan

July 9, 1936 – June 14, 2002
POET

147

LEFT BLANK ON PURPOSE

June Jordan

June Jordan

June Jordan

June Jordan

June Jordan

June Jordan

Hi, my name is June Jordan. I was born on July 9, 1936, in Harlem, NY. I attended Northfield Mount Hermon School. One of the things that I'm best known for is my commitment to human rights and political activism. Some of my works include "On a New Year's Eve," Jim Crow: The Sequel, "Poem About Process and Progress," and "In Memoriam: Martin Luther King, Jr." I published my first book, Who Look at Me, in 1969. I'm also an essayist and columnist for The Progressive. I was dedicated to respecting Black English and its usage. "There are three qualities of Black English - the presence of life, voice and clarity - that intensify to a distinctive Black value system that we became excited about and self-consciously tried to maintain."

1. Which book is one of mine?
   A. Lead From the Outside
   B. I Am Not Your Negro
   C. Jim Crow: The Sequel
2. What year did I publish my first book?
   A. 1970
   B. 1969
   C. 1968
3. What did I want everyone to respect?
   A. Each other
   B. Them selves
   C. Black English

Directions: Answer the questions, to solve the crossword puzzle. You can use the internet if you get stuck on any question.

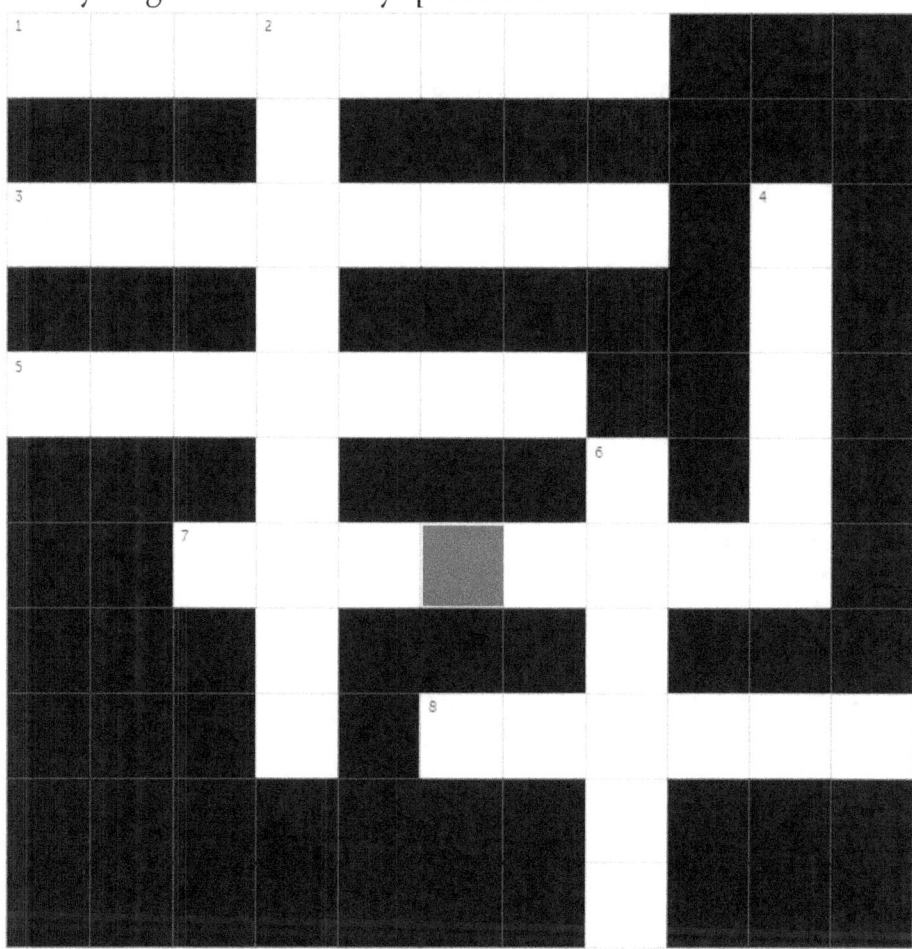

Across

1) I began my _____ career at the City College of New York.

3) I'm an American writer, poet, playwright,and _____.

5) Jordan won the Lila Wallace ____ Digest Writers Award.

7) I was a professor of English at the State University of _____.

8) June's ____ inspired her love of literature.

Down

2) June Jordan's first published book was a collection of _____ poems Who Look at Me.

4) Jordan was dedicated to respecting ___ English and its usage in her works.

6) June was the founder and director of ____ for the People at the University of California

Let learn about the style June like to write in. It is called African-American Vernacular English (AAVE), also referred to as Black English. It is the variety of English natively spoken, particularly in urban communities, by most working- and middle-class African Americans and some Black Canadians.

Here is a list of some AAVE's

1) cat 'a friend, a fellow
2) cool 'calm, controlled
3) dig 'to understand, appreciate
4) bad 'really good'
5) bad-eye 'nasty look
6) big-eye 'greedy'

Now that you have some examples to go by. Can you write down six different AAVE's.

1)   2)   3)

4)   5)   6)

If you want a bigger challenge, use your words in your own short story

Directions: Unscramble the words below about June. See if you can get the bonus word.

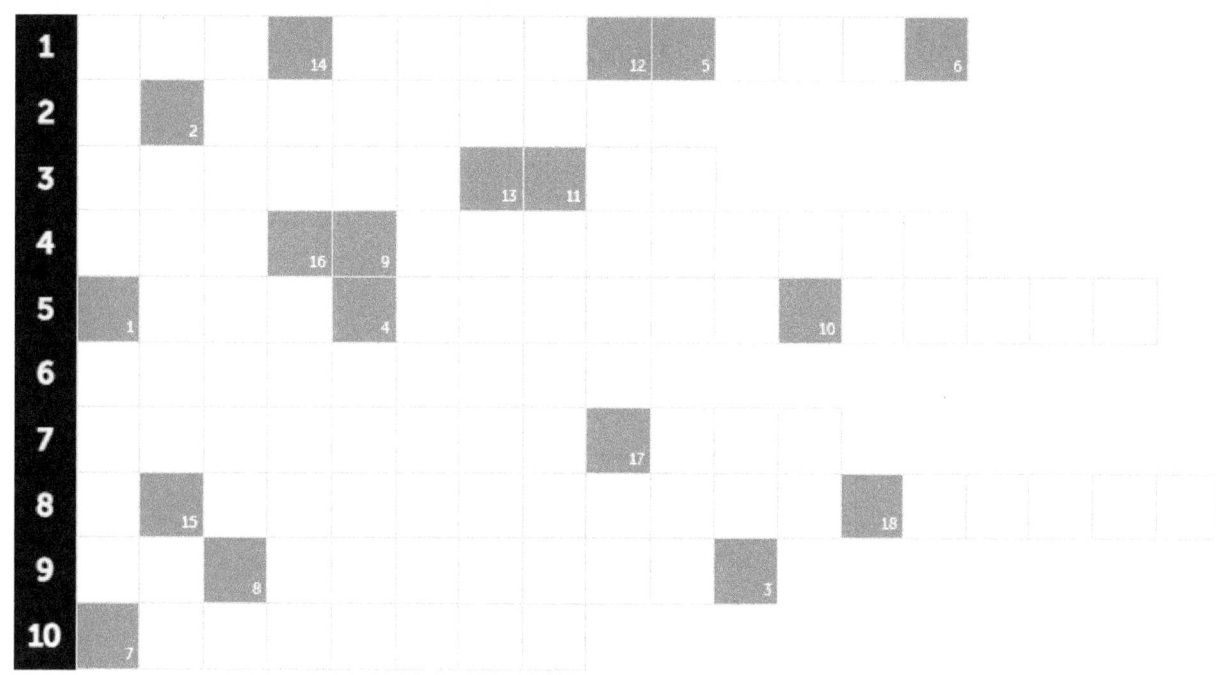

BONUS WORD

Unscramble Words

1) yeyievrualtisn   2) lsitoucnm   3) birgpoearh

4) vegrseripothse   5) ticiiaitctlvoaspl   6) ailirvcws

7) cslahkegnlib   8) beinmarctuvuiylosi   9) ooekalhmwto

10) fnemiims

Directions: This is the WGLT Challenge. Solve the cryptogram. As the puzzle solver, you need to find which number belongs to which character. And this can be pretty challenging! You will need to match the number with the letter. There are some letters given to you below. This will help you solve the other words and unlock more characters. **Good Luck.**

James Johnson

James Johnson

June 17, 1871 – June 26, 1938

WRITER/POET

155

LEFT BLANK ON PURPOSE

James Johnson

James Johnson

James Johnson

James Johnson

James Johnson

James Johnson

Hi, my name is James Johnson. I was born on June 17, 1871, in Jacksonville, FL. I attended Edwin M. Stanton School. At 16, I enrolled in Atlanta University and graduated with a bachelor's degree. I also became a member of the Phi Beta Sigma fraternity. Sticking to the motto of Phi Beta Sigma, I worked in several public capacities, including education, the diplomatic corps and civil rights activism. One of the things that I'm best known for is that I wrote "Lift Every Voice and Sing" (the Negro National Anthem), which is a title that the NAACP adopted and promoted. Some of the works I'm known for are Fifty Years and Other Poems and The Autobiography of an Ex-Colored Man. I was involved in the Harlem Renaissance of the 1920s. In 1917, I organized the famous Silent March down 5th Avenue to protest racial violence and lynching.

1. What college did I go to?
   A. Jackson State University
   B. Atlanta University
   C. Ohio State University
2. What is Life Every Voice and sing know as?
   A. The love Anthem
   B. The National Anthem
   C. The Negro National Anthem
3. How old was I when I enrolled in college?
   A. 18
   B. 16
   C. 20

Directions: Find the words associated with James's life and career.

```
D V X C I V I L R I G H T S A A F A
E R L W M Z R D T A V K F C J D F T
P R I N C I P A L N V A Q F K S J L
K H A N M Y C Z S R V U X O Z E P A
M R D A I L Y A M E R I C A N N C N
I D I N L D K K K P M S O D J O X T
C H K I P O E J X Y H D F T W B E A
K Y Y N M M O T S I L E V O N M A U
Q S I R A B X H E N I R Y Y Z O U N
U E O E Q A O R C Q K Y H L A R J I
I T M T T F C T X S M R K I W T W V
O E J I B S B P V H N Y U A P S O E
O M C R C W C J L X K O I V V D G R
K T W W V V K D F P K G T Y O O J S
T A I G R J M T O D J H Z N E G C I
O D N N H T Y M F H D L D A A A U T
Q C D O W T W C R E Y W A L O T Q Y
C C C S U N H Y N C R F P W N M S J
```

Find These Words

CIVILRIGHTS NOVELIST GODSTROMBONES
NAACP SONGWRITER ATLANTAUNIVERSITY
PRINCIPAL DAILYAMERICAN LAWYER
STANTONSCHOOL

John accomplished many things in his lifetime and in order to do that he had to set some goals. So below we will talk about what a goal is and what you should do to set your own goals.

Let's talk about Goals. A goal is something that you want to accomplish and must work towards. Sometimes reaching our goals can be a hard task. Below I want you to think of a goal that you would like to accomplish in the next year. Now before you start there are a few rules to this. First you need to make sure this goal is realistic. Second make it as specific as possible and Last but not least have a plan which I will give you the structure for below. Good Luck.

Goal #1

Now let's create steps, what I like to call stepping stones towards accomplishing those goals that we just identified as what you would like to do.

Stepping stone 1) In order to get to your goal what should you have done in the first month of your journey.

Stepping stone 2) What should you have done in the third month of your journey.

Stepping stone 3) What should you have done in the sixth month of your journey.

Stepping stone 4) What should you have done in the ninth month of your journey.

As you can see, we are checking in every 3 months to make sure we are still on task and it's always good to see if you still want to go through with what you set for yourself or if you need to make adjustments.

Directions: Read and answer the questions below. These are the different forms of poetry. There are clues in the puzzle to help you. Try and solve the cryptic message.

Clue for cryptic message: James's was a great one of these.

Questions

1) Johns founded the Daily American, the first Black-oriented daily _____ in the United States.

2) John wrote the lyrics to "Lift Every _____ and Sing," a tribute to Black endurance, hope and religious faith that was later adopted by the NAACP and dubbed "the Negro National Anthem."

3) I helped produce a six-song suite titled The Evolution of _____ that helped document and expose important Black musical idioms.

4) In 1898, I became the first Black lawyer admitted to the _____ Bar since Reconstruction.

5) I was the head of the National Association for the _____ of Colored People (NAACP) during the 1920s.

6) I worked as a professor in creative literature at _____ University.

7) In 1904, I helped write two songs for Republican candidate Theodore Roosevelt's successful _____ campaign that year.

8) Johns was the _____ writer for the New York Age, the city's oldest and most distinguished Black newspaper.

Directions: This is the WGLT Challenge. Solve the cryptogram. As the puzzle solver, you need to find which number belongs to which character. And this can be pretty challenging! You will need to match the number with the letter. There are some letters given to you below. This will help you solve the other words and unlock more characters. **Good Luck.**

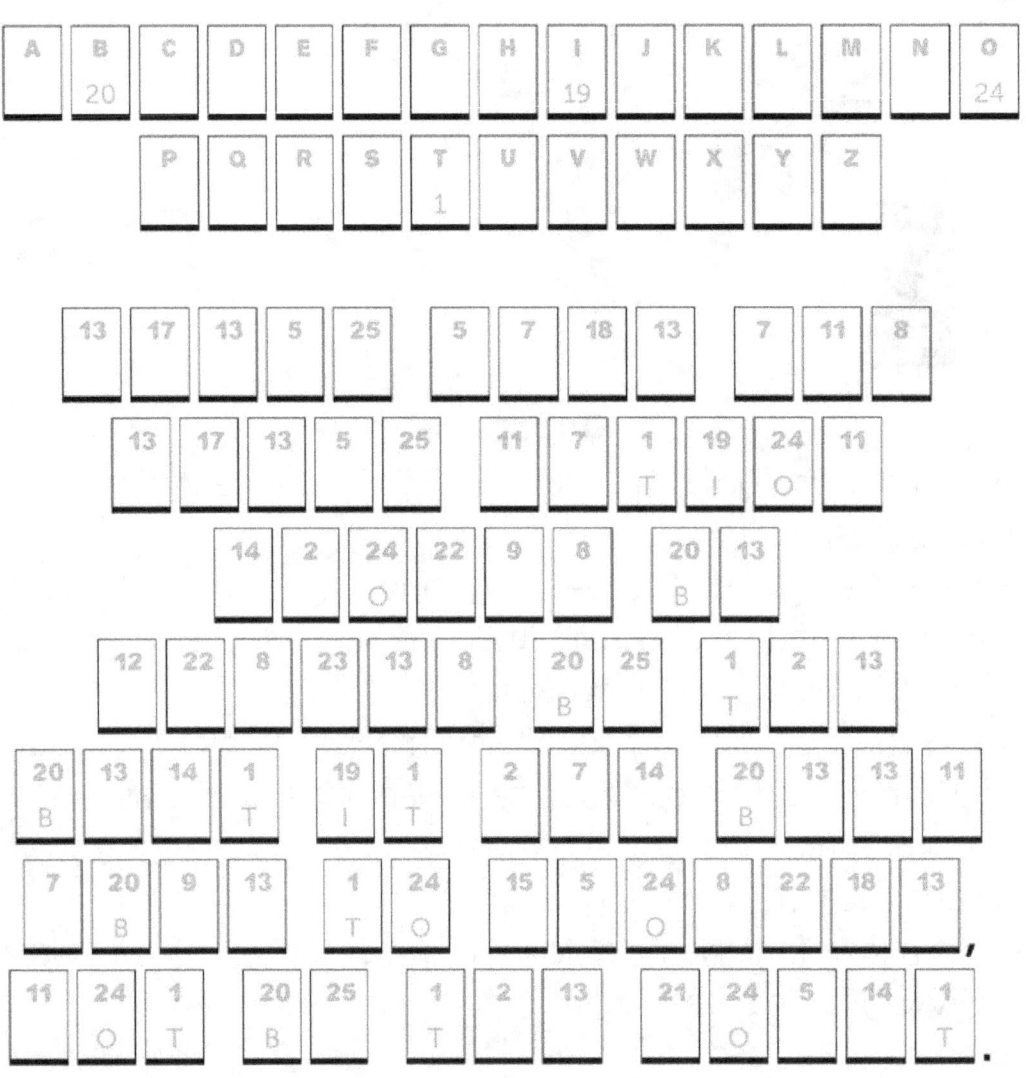

A	B	C	D	E	F	G	H	I	J	K	L	M	N	O
	20							19						24

P	Q	R	S	T	U	V	W	X	Y	Z
				1						

13	17	13	5	25		5	7	18	13		7	11	8

13	17	13	5	25	11	7	1	19	24	11
							T	I	O	

14	2	24	22	9	8		20	13
		O					B	

12	22	8	23	13	8		20	25		1	2	13
							B			T		

20	13	14	1		19	1		2	7	14		20	13	13	11
B			T		I	T						B			

7	20	9	13		1	24		15	5	24	8	22	18	13
	B				T	O				O					,

11	24	1		20	25		1	2	13		21	24	5	14	1
	O	T		B			T					O			T	.

162

Phillis Wheatley

Phillis Wheatley

1753 – December 5, 1784
AUTHOR

LEFT BLANK ON PURPOSE

Phillis Wheatley

Phillis Wheatley

Phillis Wheatley

Phillis Wheatley

Phillis Wheatley

Phillis Wheatley

Hi, my name is Phillis Wheatley. I was born in 1753 in West Africa. I was sold to a visiting trader and we traveled to Boston on a ship named Phillis. He then sold me to John Wheatley as a slave for his wife Susanna, who then gave me their last name. My first name was taken from the ship I traveled on. Even though I was a slave, Mr. and Mrs. Wheatley saw my potential and invested in me. I was able to publish my first book in 1773 at the age of 20. One of the things that I'm best known for is becoming the first American slave, the first person of African descent and the third colonial American woman to have her work published. In 1775, I sent a copy of a poem entitled "To His Excellency, George Washington" to the then-military general. He invited me to visit, which I did in March 1776.

1. How did I get my first name?
   A. From my parents
   B. From my slave owner
   C. From the ship
2. What year did I publish my first book?
   A. 1770
   B. 1774
   C. 1773
3. I was the first person of African descent to what?
   A. Come to America
   B. Have my work published
   C. Get my freedom

Directions: Answer the questions, to solve the crossword puzzle. You can use the internet if you get stuck on any question.

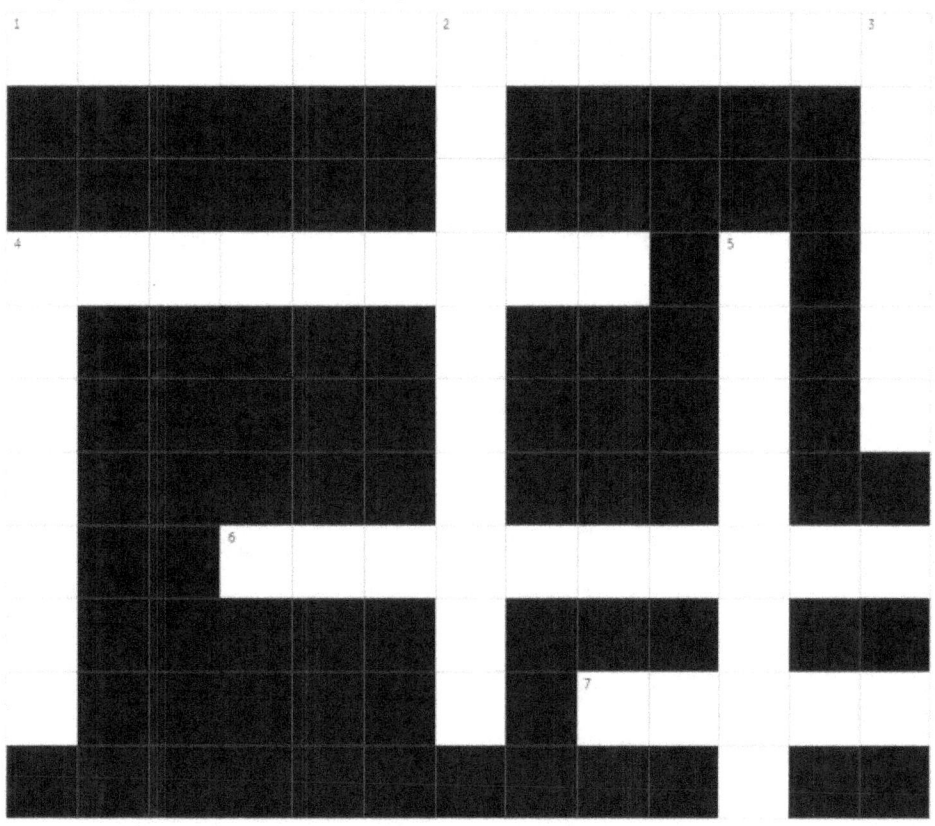

Across

1) Wheatley was the first African American to achieve an _____ reputation as a writer and earn a living through her work.

4) I was THE FIRST _____ AFRICAN-AMERICAN WOMAN.

6) In 1776, George _____ invited Phillis to visit him at his headquarters in Cambridge.

7) John Wheatley clearly stated that in his will Phillis Wheatley should be _____ after his death.

Down

2) In 1772, Wheatley was required to defend _____ of my poem in court.

3) With help from Selina Hastings, the Countess of Huntingdon, Phillis Wheatley's poetry collection was published in September 1773 in _____.

4) _____ WAS NAMED AFTER THE SLAVE SHIP THAT BROUGHT me TO U.S. and I adopted the last name of my owner John Wheatley.

5) By the time I was _____ my poems appeared in certain newspapers and periodicals in U.S. and

Directions: Read the text below. Then answer the questions that follow.

Underline the **prepositional phrase**, write whether it is being used as an **adjective** or an **adverb**

Prepositional phrases can: act like an adjective and describe a noun
can: act line an adverb and describe how, when, or where something takes place.

_____**1.)** Our trip will be in Cambridgeshire, England.

_____**2.)** The girl in the pink pants asked me to play

basketball

_____ **3.)** Did you see the boy in the window?

_____**4.)** The books behind the stairs are not mine.

_____5.) My uncle works out after breakfast

_____**6.)** Under the bed, we hid all of our Christmas gifts.

_____**7.)** The man behind my mom is my uncle.

_____ **8.)** My mom travels by train when she works.

Directions: Unscramble the words below about Phillis. See if you can get the bonus word.

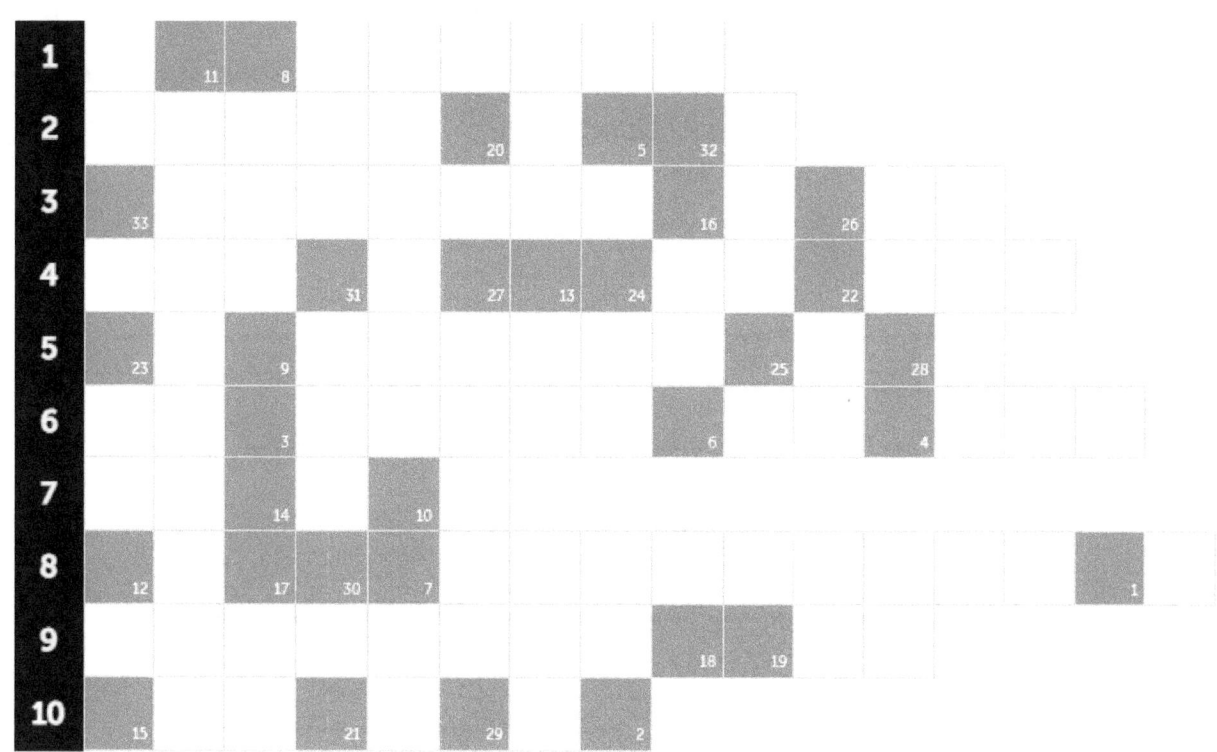

BONUS WORD

Unscramble Words

1) ilbpushed

2) wafistcera

3) apnpaxdeleore

4) ashtnslgiaseni

5) moachcsnriaht

6) rlpnaiecybdteae

7) arhotu

8) girngeoshgaoetwn

9) llucramydesi

10) uertnfoe

Directions: This is the WGLT Challenge. Solve the cryptogram. As the puzzle solver, you need to find which number belongs to which character. And this can be pretty challenging! You will need to match the number with the letter. There are some letters given to you below. This will help you solve the other words and unlock more characters. **Good Luck.**

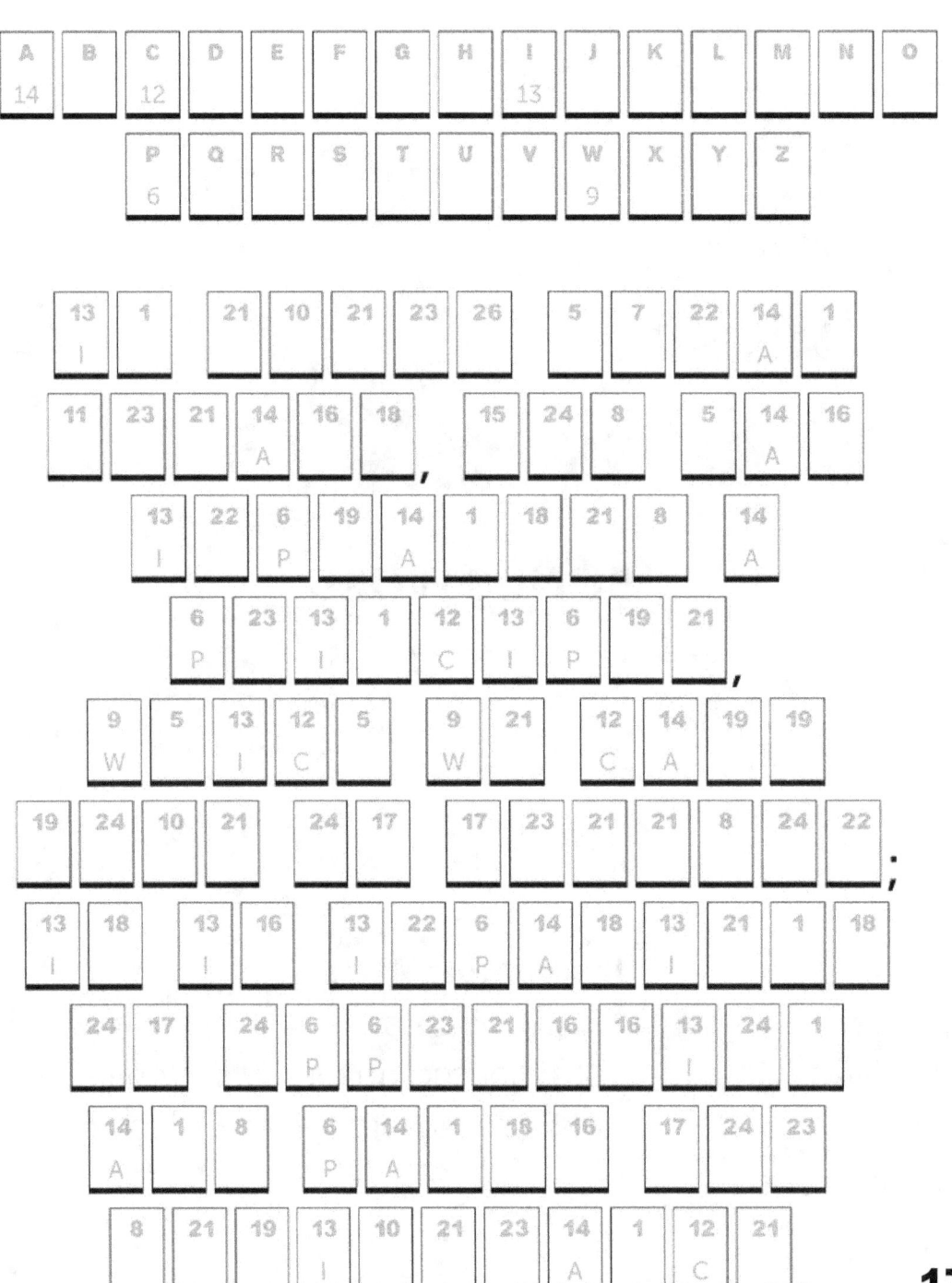

A	B	C	D	E	F	G	H	I	J	K	L	M	N	O
14		12						13						

P	Q	R	S	T	U	V	W	X	Y	Z
6							9			

Claude McKay

Claude McKay

September 15, 1890 – May 22, 1948

WRITER/POET

171

Claude McKay

Claude McKay

Claude McKay

Claude McKay

Claude McKay

Claude McKay

Hi, my name is Festus Claudius McKay. I was born on September 15, 1890, in Nairne Castle in upper Clarendon Parish, Jamaica. I attended Tuskegee University, but due to intense racism, I left and went to Kansas State University. I published my first book of poems, Songs of Jamaica, in 1912. I was a key figure in the Harlem Renaissance, which was a prominent literary movement of the 1920s. My work ranged from vernacular verse that celebrated peasant life in Jamaica to poems that protested racial and economic inequities. Some of the works that I'm known for are Home to Harlem, Gingertown, A Long Way from Home and Harlem: Negro Metropolis.

1. **What year did I publish my first book?**
   A. **1912**
   B. **1909**
   C. **1912**
2. **What University didn't I attend?**
   A. **Tuskegee University**
   B. **Kansas State University**
   C. **Howard University**
3. **What is not one of my books?**
   A. **A Long Way from Home**
   B. **Invisible Man**
   C. **Home to Harlem**

Directions: Find the words associated with Claude's life and career.

```
H  M  U  H  Q  Q  E  Z  G  W  D  G  A  C  B  H  D  B
M  A  X  Q  U  I  T  X  H  U  U  P  C  T  B  Q  Z  Y
Q  O  R  P  E  L  I  E  D  W  A  R  D  S  Q  R  S  B
C  M  P  L  P  K  P  L  K  F  H  Q  S  G  N  T  L  W
C  Q  R  A  E  U  R  T  L  Z  H  F  X  T  W  O  T  X
H  B  F  O  L  M  Y  C  C  Y  U  R  A  D  N  S  C  K
N  K  G  O  T  L  R  O  S  H  R  O  Z  D  O  Z  W  O
V  S  J  C  F  A  E  E  W  G  X  J  O  S  U  C  V  D
J  R  Q  C  P  B  R  V  N  N  S  N  U  J  X  V  I  E
J  U  K  O  F  U  N  E  O  A  U  V  Q  X  L  T  N  T
N  S  P  R  O  R  R  P  B  N  I  W  W  H  X  X  U  A
Y  S  V  O  T  E  Y  K  U  I  T  S  G  V  C  N  Y  G
H  I  N  M  M  O  B  B  F  I  L  J  S  E  L  S  F  E
O  A  A  Z  K  F  Y  H  C  F  E  E  I  A  S  E  M  R
I  C  Z  H  A  M  X  P  J  K  L  V  H  N  N  D  P  G
S  O  W  V  J  N  Q  P  Q  F  E  A  V  T  V  C  Y  E
X  Z  U  N  S  T  E  N  N  O  S  I  J  B  Y  L  E  S
T  U  S  K  E  G  E  E  I  N  S  T  I  T  U  T  E  O
```

Find These Words

HARLEMRENAISSANCE	NOVELLA	THELIBERATOR
TUSKEGEEINSTITUTE	SEGREGATED	ELIEDWARDS
LONDON	RUSSIA	SONNETS
MOROCCO		

175

Directions: Rewrite the verbs in the correct column (Past/ Present/ Future)

Past tense and past progressive: I watched. I was watching.

Present tense and present progressive: I watch. I am watching.

Future tense and future progressive: I will watch. I will be watching.

walked	will drink	bought	will greet	was eating
ate	is jogging	is playing	will be sliding	was touching
catch	will drive	begin	pull	will teach

Past	Present	Future

176

Directions: Read and answer the questions below. These are the different forms of poetry. There are clues in the puzzle to help you. Try and solve the cryptic message.

Clue for cryptic message: Claude's ventured around these parts.

Questions

1) Claude was an _____ figure in the Harlem Renaissance.

2) I studied at _____ Institute when I first got to the United States.

3) McKay wrote poems challenging the state of affairs on _____.

4) "If We Must Die", was published in my magazine _____.

5) A London _____ house produced Claude's first books of verse, Songs of Jamaica.

6) _____ Claudius McKay was born in Clarendon Parish, Jamaica.

Directions: This is the WGLT Challenge. Solve the cryptogram. As the puzzle solver, you need to find which number belongs to which character. And this can be pretty challenging! You will need to match the number with the letter. There are some letters given to you below. This will help you solve the other words and unlock more characters. **Good Luck.**

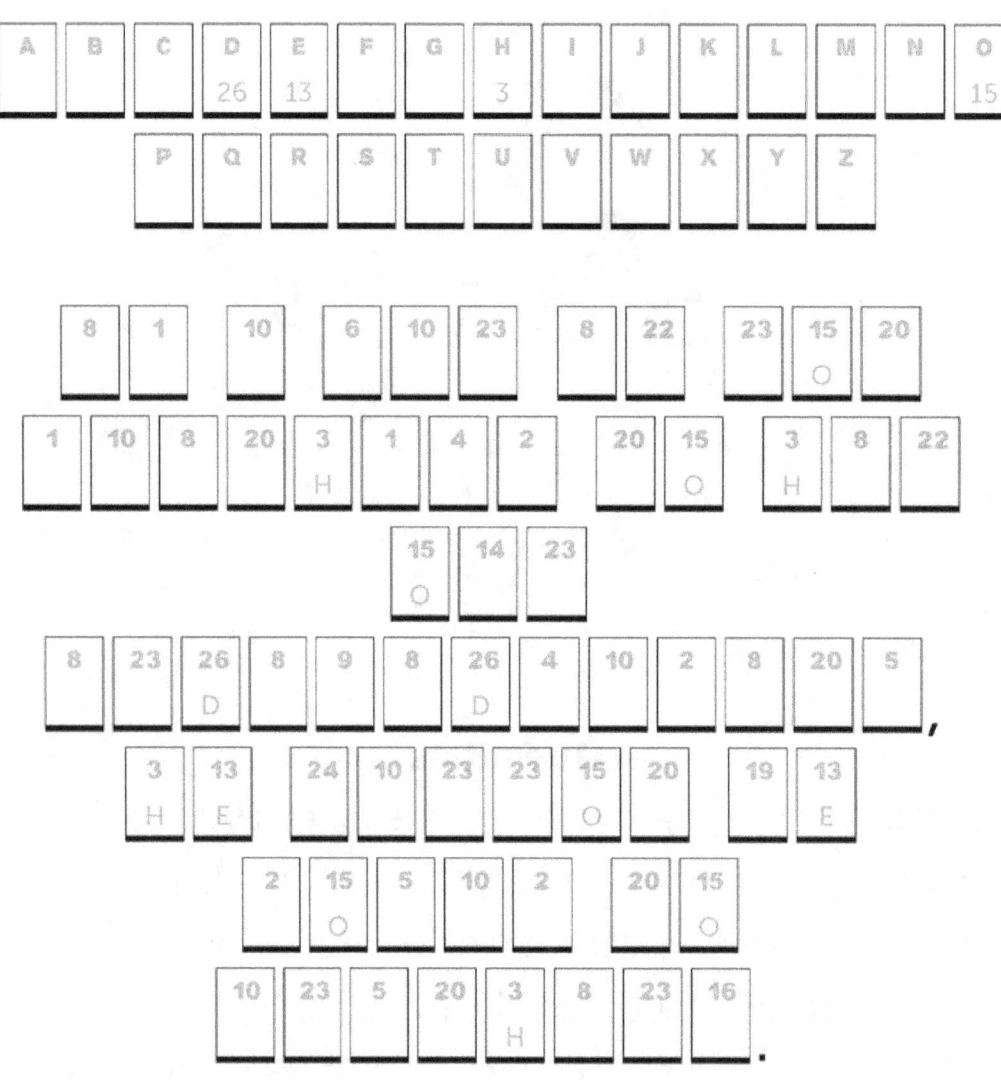

A	B	C	D	E	F	G	H	I	J	K	L	M	N	O
			26	13			3							15

P	Q	R	S	T	U	V	W	X	Y	Z

| 8 | 1 | 10 | 6 | 10 | 23 | 8 | 22 | 23 | 15 (O) | 20 |

| 1 | 10 | 8 | 20 | 3 (H) | 1 | 4 | 2 | 20 | 15 (O) | 3 (H) | 8 | 22 |

| 15 (O) | 14 | 23 |

| 8 | 23 | 26 (D) | 8 | 9 | 8 | 26 (D) | 4 | 10 | 2 | 8 | 20 | 5 |,

| 3 (H) | 13 (E) | 24 | 10 | 23 | 23 | 15 (O) | 20 | 19 | 13 (E) |

| 2 | 15 (O) | 5 | 10 | 2 | 20 | 15 (O) |

| 10 | 23 | 5 | 20 | 3 (H) | 8 | 23 | 16 |.

Nikki Giovanni

Nikki Giovanni

June 7, 1943 – Present
WRITER/POET

179

Nikki Giovanni

Nikki Giovanni

Nikki Giovanni

Nikki Giovanni

Nikki Giovanni

Nikki Giovanni

Hi, my name is Yolande Cornelia Nikki Giovanni Jr. I was born on June 7, 1943, in Knoxville, TN. I attended Austin High School. I graduated from Fisk University with a bachelor's in history. I was one of the foremost authors of the Black Arts Movement. Influenced by the civil rights movement and the Black Power movement of the period, my early work provides a strong, militant African American perspective. Some of my works include Black Feeling, Black Talk/Black Judgment, Make Me Rain: Poems and Prose, The Nikki Giovanni Poetry Collection and 100 Best African American Poems. I was teaching at Virginia Tech in 2007 when a former student of mine killed 32 people. I was asked to give a convocation speech, which I did. I was able to unite the nation that day.

1. What University did I graduate from?
   A. Jackson State
   B. Spellman
   C. Fisk
2. What inspired some of my work?
   A. College
   B. Civil Rights Movement
   C. Growing Up
3. What city was I born in?
   A. Knoxville
   B. Scranton
   C. Philadelphia

Directions: Answer the questions, to solve the crossword puzzle. You can use the internet if you get stuck on any question.

Across

3) Nikki got her Master's degree in poetry from _____ University.

4) Nikki got a Bachelor's Degree from _____ University.

5) I was a part of the Black ___ Movement.

8) Nikki was named Woman of the year by _____ magazine.

Down

1) Nikki use to teach at _____ University in New Jersey.

2) Nikki is a Distinguished Professor in the Department of English at _____ University.

6) Nikki was a keynote speaker at _____ University.

7) Nikki was a regular on the T.V. program _____.

Directions: Combine the sentences into one sentence. Separate items in a list with commas.

1) Brutus is my pet. Trixie is also my pet. Mary is also my pet.

2) The uncle went to shop. The kids went to shop. The parents also went to shop.

3) She was sad because she lost her purse. She also failed her driving test. Then she forgot her mom's dinner.

4) We bought a candy. We bought some food too. We bought some drinks as well.

5) Amy is my cousin. Matt is also my cousin. Nikki is my cousin too.

6) This pot is hot. It is also big. It is dirty too.

7) My dad eats ham. He eats eggs too. He eats grits also.

8) This poet writes. She lectures as well. She also teaches.:

Directions: Unscramble the words below about Nikki. See if you can get the bonus word.

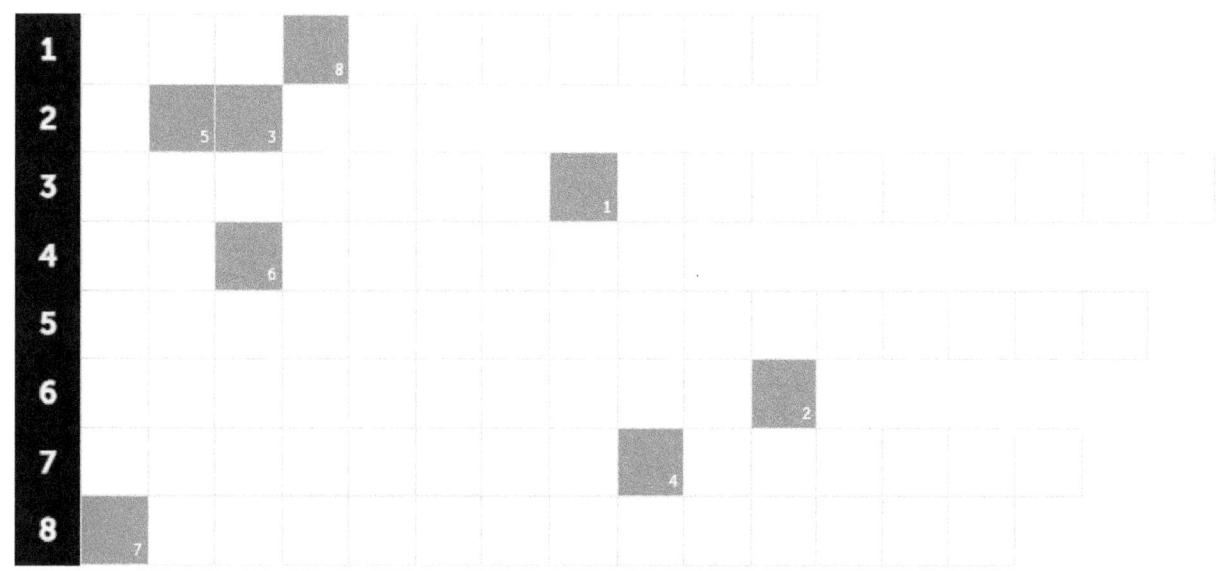

BONUS WORD

1	2	3	4		5	6	7	8

Unscramble Words

1) eoenmsyllea

2) ubels

3) clsmkeoatnmvtbrae

4) hiesatoot

5) stkitohemrhraesy

6) ratiievhngc

7) amaaadrpenwcaig

8) uyivitssefkrin

Directions: This is the WGLT Challenge. Solve the cryptogram. As the puzzle solver, you need to find which number belongs to which character. And this can be pretty challenging! You will need to match the number with the letter. There are some letters given to you below. This will help you solve the other words and unlock more characters. **Good Luck.**

Paul Dunbar

Paul Dunbar

June 27, 1872 – February 9, 1906

POET

187

Paul Dunbar

Paul Dunbar

Paul Dunbar

Paul Dunbar

Paul Dunbar

Paul Dunbar

Directions: read the bio below and answer the following questions.

Hi, my name is Paul Dunbar. I was born on June 27, 1872, in Dayton, OH. I attended Central High School in Dayton. I was the only African American student and airplane co-inventor Orville Wright was my classmate and friend. I was the first writer to put the African American experience in all its diverse forms before a broader audience. Some of my works include Majors and Minors, Lyrics of Lowly Life, "Sympathy," and Candle-Lightin' Time. I was one of the first African American poets to gain national recognition for using dialectic verse in my collections. After my death, my mother, Matilda, opened up my house on my birthday and after her death, the state of Ohio purchased the house. It became my memorial. My house was the first state memorial to an African American in the nation.

1. Who was my classmate in High School?
   A. Frederick Douglass
   B. Orville Wright
   C. James Johnson
2. What made my work unique?
   A. Metaphors
   B. Dialectic
   C. My use of Haiku
3. What city was my High Shool in?
   A. Columbus
   B. Youngstown
   C. Dayton

Directions: Find the words associated with Paul's life and career.

```
Q  X  W  C  V  S  Y  T  S  I  L  E  V  O  N  Y  Y  U
K  E  L  E  V  A  T  O  R  O  P  E  R  A  T  O  R  K
P  T  S  Y  C  A  O  A  I  U  U  F  Z  K  N  C  D  I
D  Z  K  R  Z  X  J  U  W  Z  E  B  X  Y  I  W  H  R
J  M  M  G  E  O  V  T  Q  B  N  V  W  N  N  U  J  C
N  Z  U  C  T  I  P  E  S  Q  S  O  D  G  W  B  B  W
S  A  T  D  A  W  D  Y  L  O  V  A  U  Y  P  L  A  R
I  J  D  T  X  G  W  L  N  L  H  V  V  Z  S  H  Z  T
S  P  R  V  F  C  D  H  O  O  Z  I  B  M  F  S  D  M
O  Y  V  E  E  L  B  X  M  S  D  T  N  P  M  S  V  D
L  E  W  Q  L  Z  L  E  N  N  D  J  N  E  B  Q  G  E
U  O  T  K  P  T  Y  P  A  W  X  E  C  R  X  Q  S  P
C  N  H  U  K  F  T  K  O  K  O  J  R  V  U  L  A  S
R  D  N  P  F  T  A  A  O  E  F  I  Q  Y  H  U  K  K
E  J  X  L  V  O  X  X  T  G  T  Z  N  A  T  Z  V  M
B  T  X  L  A  I  V  C  Q  E  D  R  J  J  N  R  X  M
U  S  E  B  Y  A  K  Y  R  K  H  B  Y  S  S  Z  A  T
T  M  Z  M  K  W  C  X  X  O  H  T  Q  X  M  B  W  M
```

Find These Words

POETRY	MARTYREDSOLDIERS	THETATTLER
OAKANDIVY	ELEVATOROPERATOR	INDAHOMEY
TUBERCULOSIS	NOVELIST	

Directions: Circle the **pronoun** in the sentence. Write the type of **pronoun**. A **possessive pronoun** refers to a specific owner: mine, yours, my, hers, his, its, your. A **relative pronoun** connects a phrase to a noun/ pronoun: who, which, that, whom. An **indefinite pronoun** doesn't refer to anything specific: all, any, each, some, several.

1) My car is the freshest on the block.

2) Are some adults taking the bus to the museum?

3) The cat that chases mice lives behind the grocery store.

4) The movie that Paul saw was outstanding.

5) We let our snake run free for the morning.

6) The purse is mine.

7) Each player has to buy a uniform and sneakers.

8) Some students are going to the party after the football game.

Directions: Read and answer the questions below. These are the different forms of poetry. There are clues in the puzzle to help you. Try and solve the cryptic message.

Clue for cryptic message: This is one of Paul's novels he created.

Questions

1) My high school classmates Wilbur and Orville _____.

2) Dunbar attended _____ University.

3) Paul started publicly reciting his poetry at the age of _____.

4) Paul's wife Alice graduated from Straight _____ (now Dillard University).

5) Dunbar traveled the world and got to meet the Queen of _____.

6) Paul Dunbar was the only _____ student in his graduating class at Central High School in Dayton.

7) Paul Dunbar house was the first state _____ to an African-American in the nation.

8) Paul has a school in Dayton called Paul Laurence Dunbar Early _____ High School.

9) Paul's nickname was "_____ boy poet."

10) Paul worked as a clerk for the library of _____.

11) Paul Dunbar died on the word _____ while reciting the 23th Psalms. **193**

Directions: This is the WGLT Challenge. Solve the cryptogram. As the puzzle solver, you need to find which number belongs to which character. And this can be pretty challenging! You will need to match the number with the letter. There are some letters given to you below. This will help you solve the other words and unlock more characters. **Good Luck.**

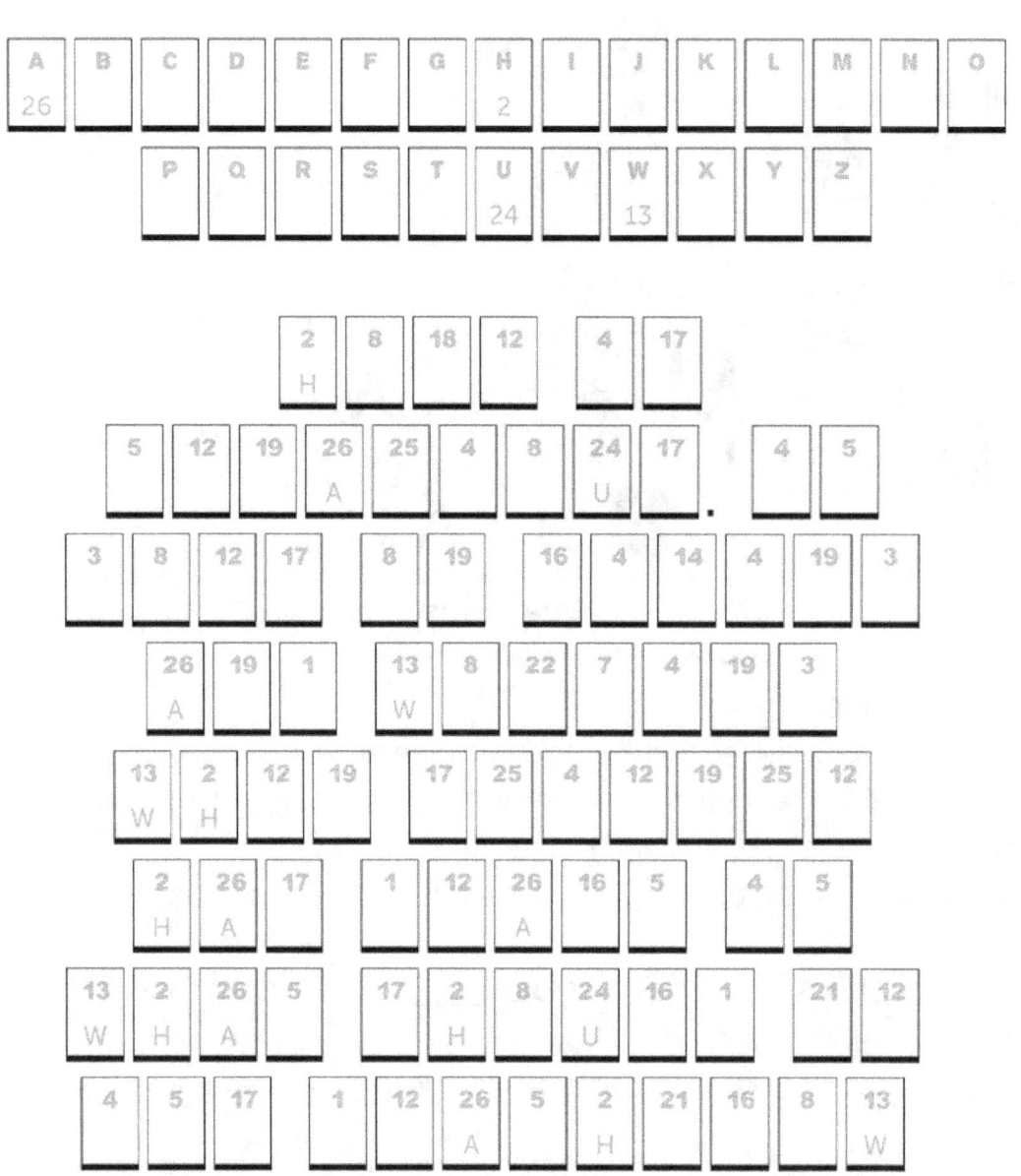

A	B	C	D	E	F	G	H	I	J	K	L	M	N	O
26							2							

P	Q	R	S	T	U	V	W	X	Y	Z
					24		13			

2	8	18	12		4	17
H						

5	12	19	26	25	4	8	24	17		4	5
			A				U				

.

3	8	12	17		8	19		16	4	14	4	19	3

26	19	1		13	8	22	7	4	19	3
A				W						

13	2	12	19		17	25	4	12	19	25	12
W	H										

2	26	17		1	12	26	16	5		4	5
H	A					A					

13	2	26	5		17	2	8	24	16	1		21	12
W	H	A				H		U					

4	5	17		1	12	26	5	2	21	16	8	13
						A		H				W

James Van Der Zee

James Van Der Zee

June 29, 1886 – May 15, 1983
PHOTOGRAPHER

195

LEFT BLANK ON PURPOSE

James Van Der Zee

James Van Der Zee

James Van Der Zee

James Van Der Zee

James Van Der Zee

James Van Der Zee

Hi, my name is James Van Der Zee. I was born on June 29, 1886, in Lenox, MA. I had a gift for music and aspired to be a professional violinist. I got my first camera when I was a teenager and photography became my second love. One of the things that I'm best known for is my detailed imagery of African American life and photographing celebrities such as Florence Mills, Joe Louis, Bojangles Robinson and Marcus Garvey. I was the official photographer for Garvey's Universal Negro Improvement Association (UNIA) Parade. The Metropolitan Museum of Art in NY featured an exhibition called "Harlem on My Mind," which featured 90% of my work. Some of the exhibitions I'm featured in are located at the Studio Museum, Lenox Library, San Francisco Museum of Modern Art and Landesmuseum. During the 1920s and 1930s, I became known as the "eyes of Harlem."

1. What did I first aspire to be?
   A. Photographer
   B. Pianist
   C. Violinist
2. What years did I become know as the eyes of Harlem?
   A. 1920s
   B. 1910s
   C. 1930s
3. What parade did I capture pictures for?
   A. Macy Day
   B. Universal Negro Improvement Association
   C. Memorial Day

Directions: Answer the questions, to solve the crossword puzzle. You can use the internet if you get stuck on any question.

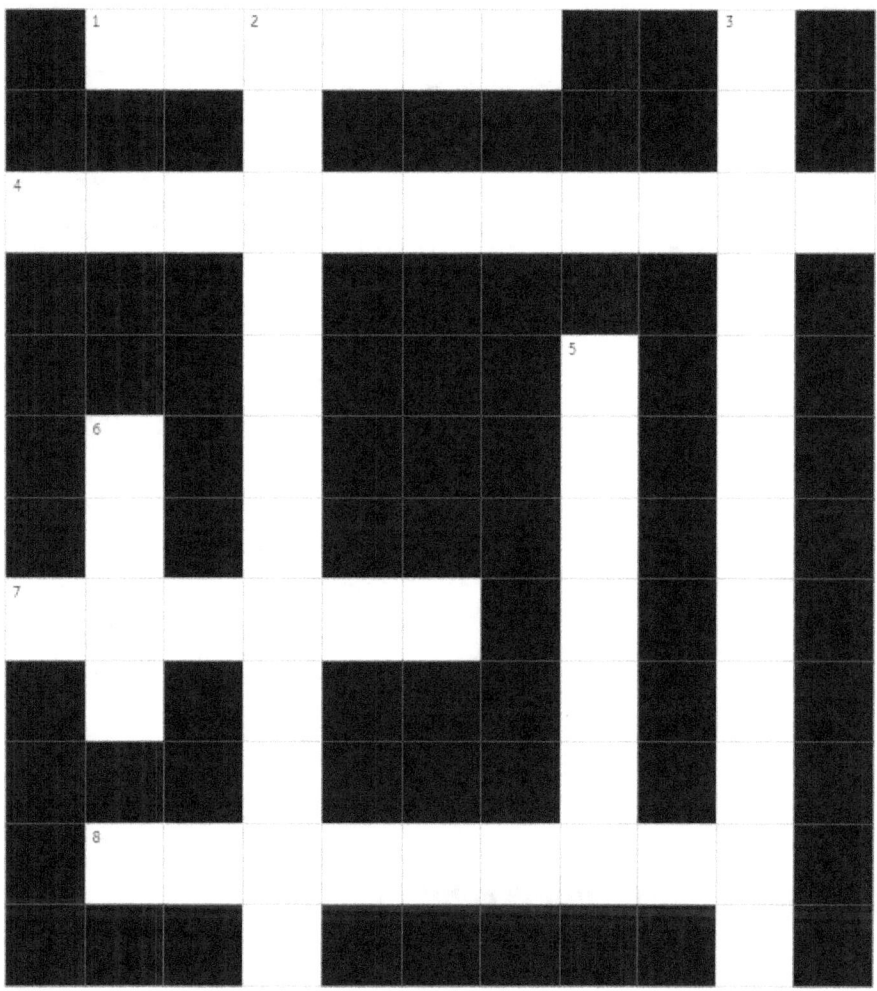

Across

1) It all started when I entered a magazine promotion to win a _____, which he won.

4) During The Great Depression James added photo _____ services to his business.

7) James co-founded the _____ Orchestra.

8) In 1918, James established the _____ Photo Studio in Harlem.

Down

2) James provided the majority of the art work for the _____ Museum of Art, New York exhibition "Harlem on My Mind."

3) Early in James's career, he gained experience as a portrait _____.

5) James was a skilled pianist and aspiring professional violinist.

6) In 1978, James published The Harlem Book of the _____.

Directions: Circle the verbs in the sentences. **Verbs** are doing words. A verb can express a physical action, a mental action or a state of being.

1) I ordered a hamburger with egg and mushrooms.

2) The lion scared me and I screamed for help.

3) I reached for the ring on the glass shelf.

4) James picked up the key and threw it to Sophia.

5) First you measure the milk, then you pour it in a bowl.

6) When I am happy, I sing a funny song.

7) The dog barked at the mailman on the sidewalk.

8) The waiter served us tea and pizza.

9) We all watched the last episode together.

10) There were no seats at the museum, so we stood.

Directions: Unscramble the words below about James. See if you can get the bonus word.

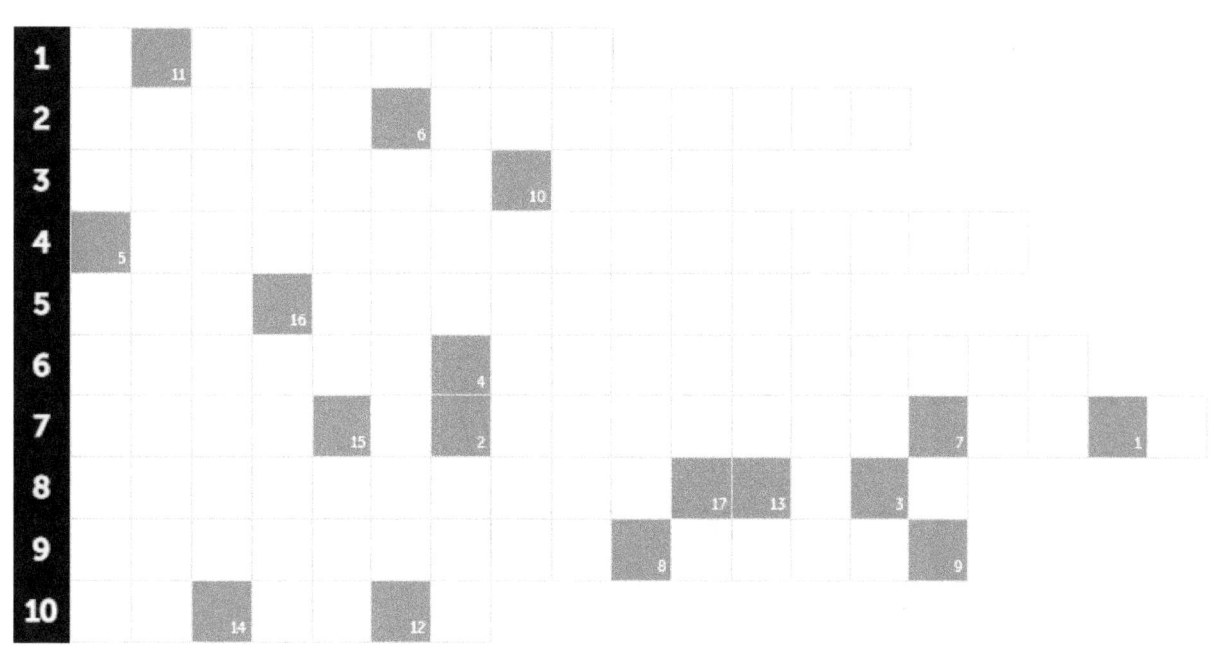

BONUS WORD

1	2	3	4	5	6	7	8	9	10	11	12	13	14	15	16	17

Unscramble Words

1) iionlitsv

2) hmnnmmlrioeyad

3) opthraygoph

4) povoterrataoelre

5) mruraygercasv

6) esonnbbnlsiaojrgo

7) racghpylenatoopadhr

8) roehcesmthraarl

9) geisadsreorpetn

10) pstniia

Directions: This is the WGLT Challenge. Solve the cryptogram. As the puzzle solver, you need to find which number belongs to which character. And this can be pretty challenging! You will need to match the number with the letter. There are some letters given to you below. This will help you solve the other words and unlock more characters. **Good Luck.**

1. **Where was I born?**
   A. Chicago, IL
   B. Atlanta, GA
   C. Brooklyn, NY
2. **I became the first African American woman to exhibit at?**
   A. Manifesta
   B. Venice Biennale
   C. Whitney Biennial
3. **Name a city where my art was featured at?**
   A. Chicago
   B. Los Angeles
   C. Orlando

Answer Key

1. canvas
2. camera
3. depth
4. museum
5. Painting
6. portrait
7. exhibition
8. gallery
9. Imagery
10. cenery

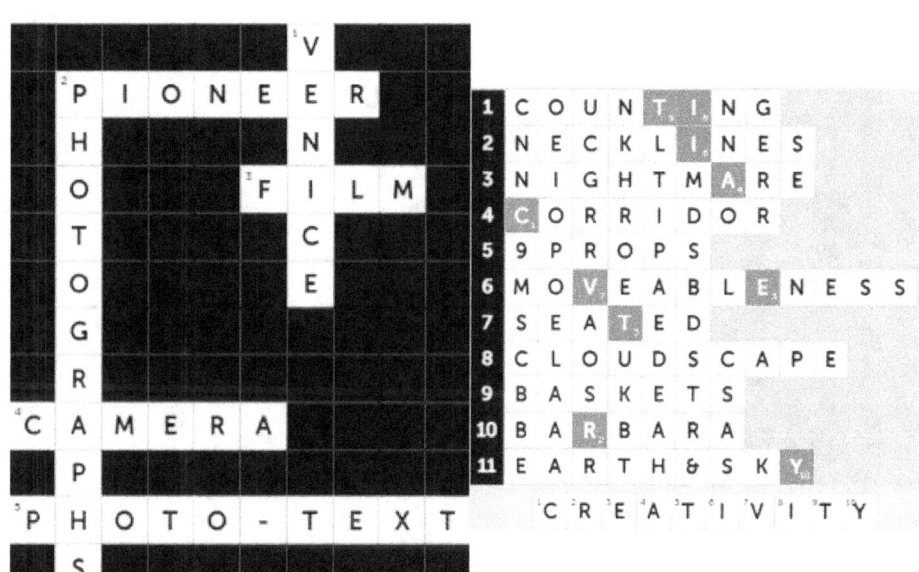

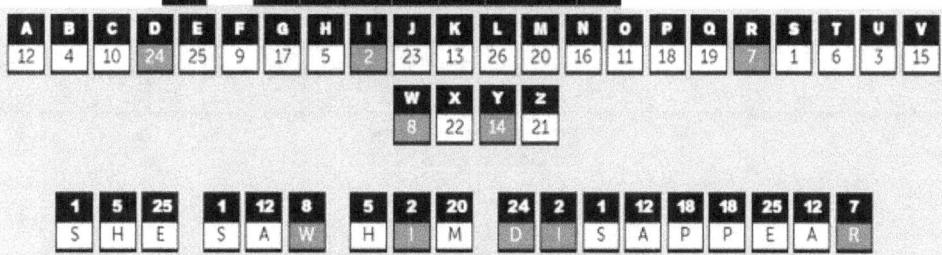

1. **Where was I born?**
   A. Brooklyn, NY
   B. Orlando, FL
   C. Portland, OR
2. **Who inspired me to publish my first book?**
   A. W.B Yeats
   B. Gwendolyn Brooks
   C. Sylvia Plath
3. **What is my Master of Arts degree in?**
   A. Poetry
   B. Medical
   C. English

Poem form answers

1) B. Style
2) B. Refers to its structure
3) C. Form

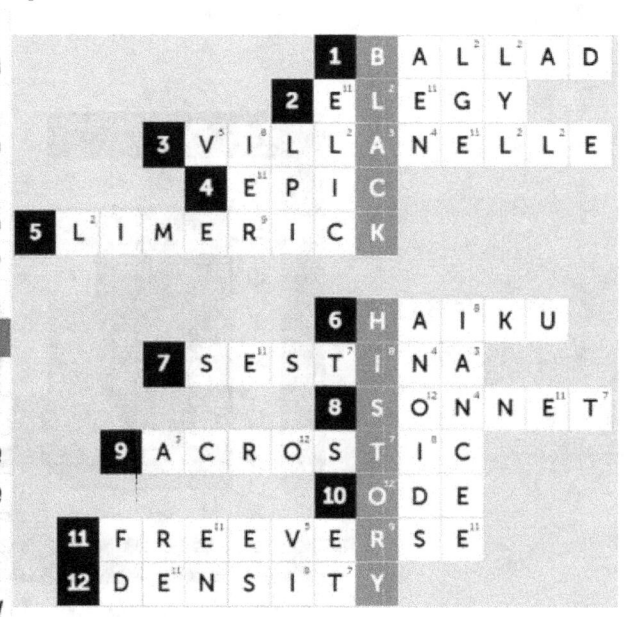

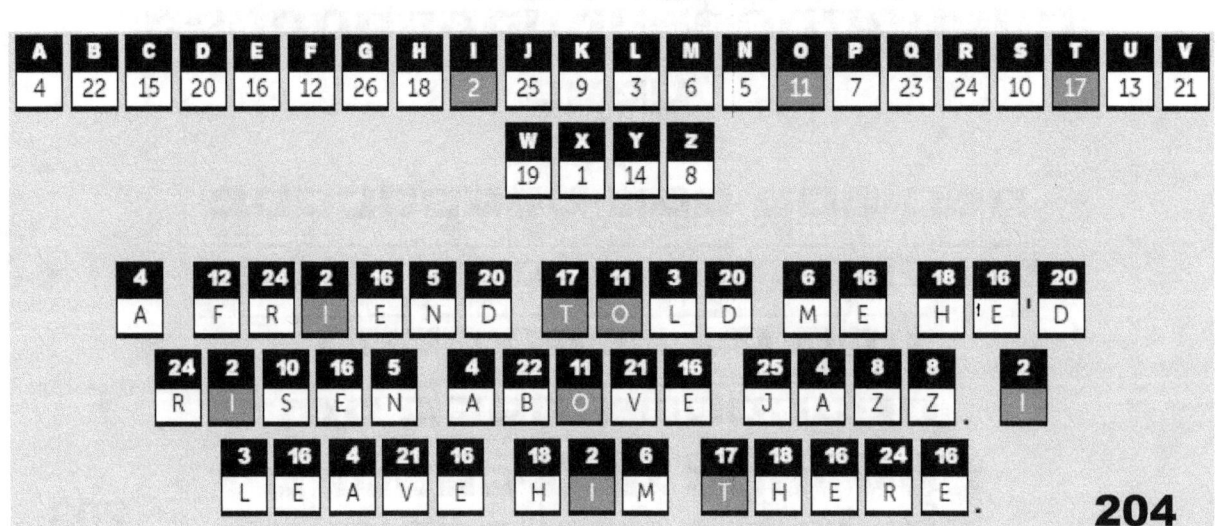

1. **Which poem is not mine?**
   A. **Coal**
   B. Notes of a Native Son
   C. **The Black Unicorn**
2. **What does Gamba Adisa mean?**
   A. Warrior
   B. **Soldier**
   C. **Gladiator**
3. **Where was I born?**
   A. **Brooklyn, NY**
   B. Harlem, New York, NY
   C. **Columbus, OH**

Synonyms questions and answers

1) disorganization
2) inability
3) prose
4) milky
5) future
6) prose
7) solid
8) original
9) silence
10) dissimilarity

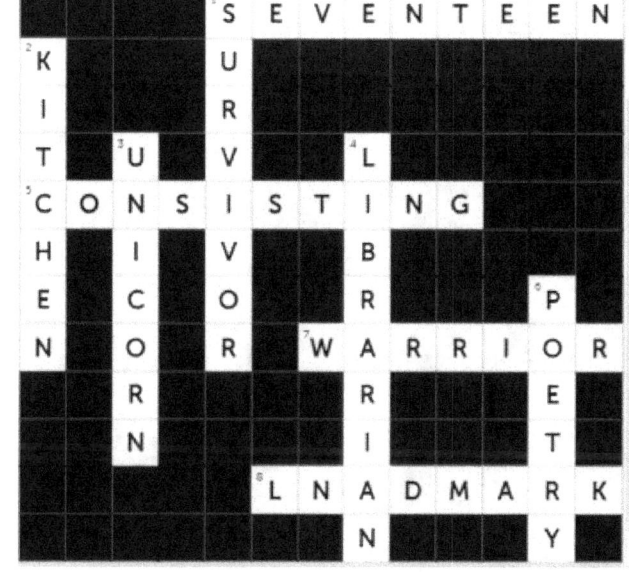

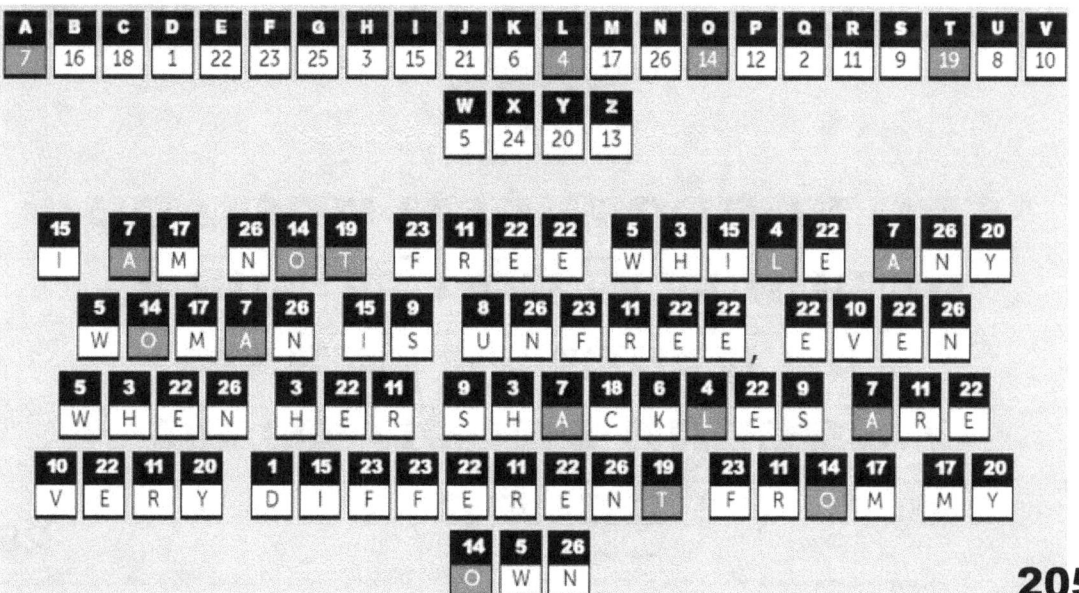

1. **How old was I when I moved to Paris?**
   A. 27
   B. 24
   C. 30
2. **What was the name of my High School Magazine?**
   A. The Gazette
   B. The New Yorker
   C. The Magpie
3. **Which work of art is not my own?**
   A. Notes of a Native Son
   B. Still I Rise
   C. Giovanni's Room

Geography answers

Senegal Africa
Löeche-les-Bains Europe
Sierra Leone Africa
Istanbul Asia / Europe
New York North America
Paris Europe
Guinea Africa
Washington D.C. North America
Liberia Africa
Ghana Africa

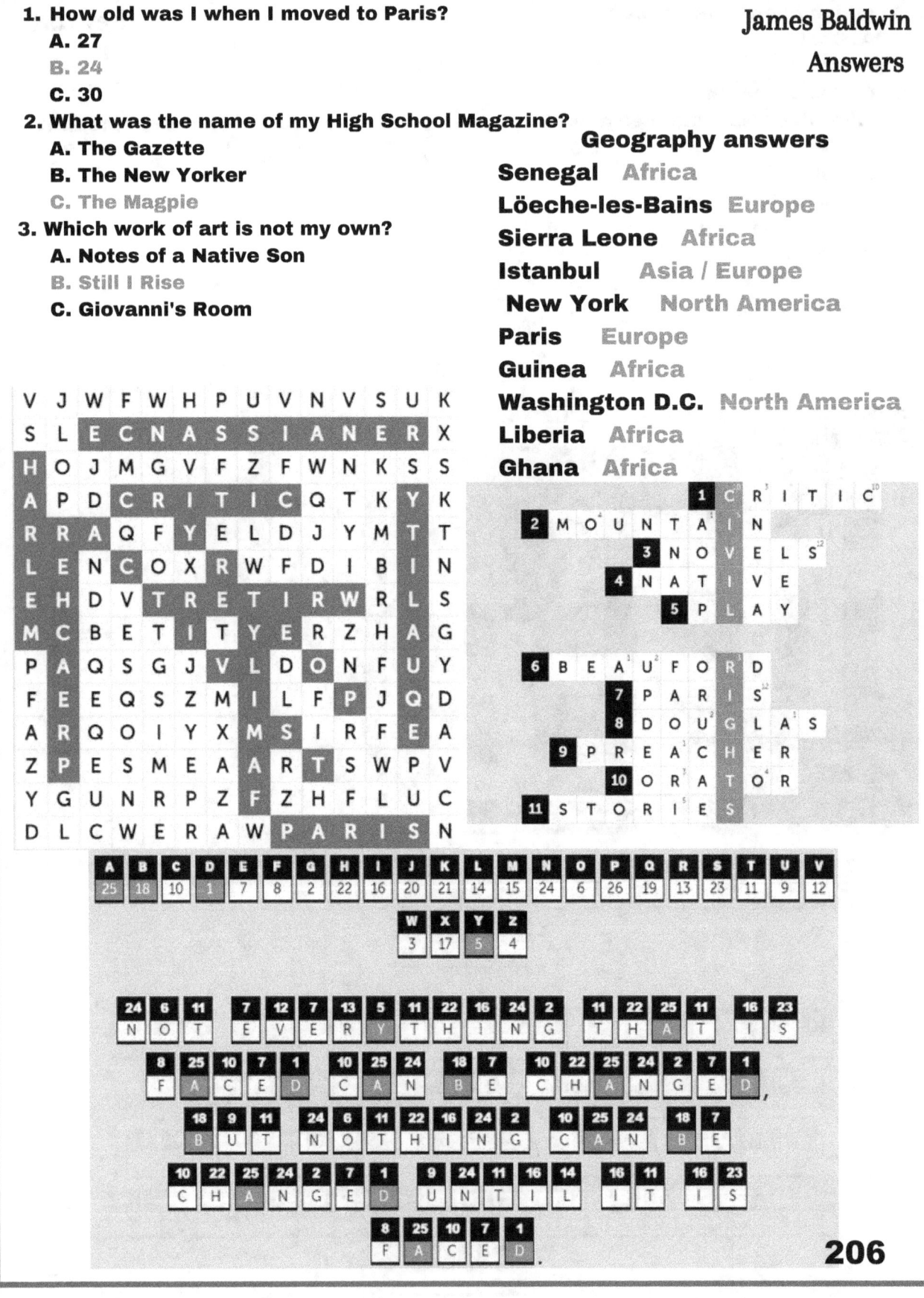

1. **What state was I born in?**
   A. Texas
   B. Florida
   C. Ohio
2. **What was the name of my work for my first commission?**
   A. Marcus Garvey
   B. Gamin
   C. W.E.B. Du Bois
3. **Which work of art is mine?**
   A. The Tom Tom
   B. Sadness
   C. Head of a Negro Boy

Additive sculpting
Model Magic
Plasticine Clay
Polymer Clay
Air Dry Clay

Subtractive sculpting
Soap Sculpture
Plaster of Paris
Balsa Wood

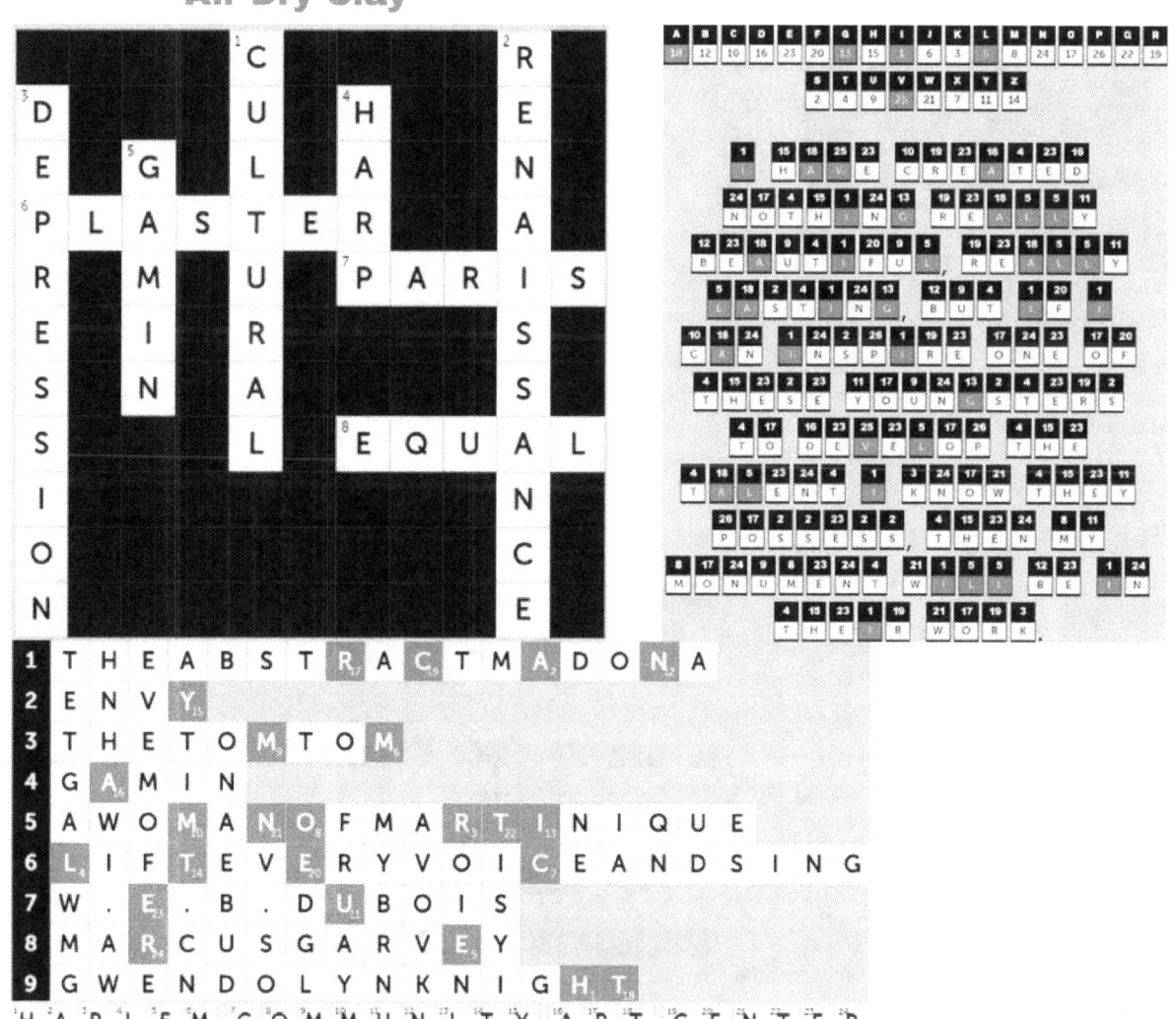

1. Who's assassination caused me change my name?
   A. Martin Luther King Jr
   B. Malcolm X
   C. Medgar Evers
2. What was the name of my High School?
   A. Ross High School
   B. DeWitt Clinton High School
   C. Barringer High School
3. Which rank was I in the military?
   A. Sergeant Major
   B. Sergeant First Class
   C. Sergeant

Possessive noun

Amiri's books
teachers' papers
Obalaji's canvas
student's pencil
friends' jacket

Rewrite Sentence Answers

They are Sue's pants.
It is the Jones' flute.
It is the doll's hat.
It is the Barakas' house.
It is Kellie's mask.
They are Lisa's sandals.

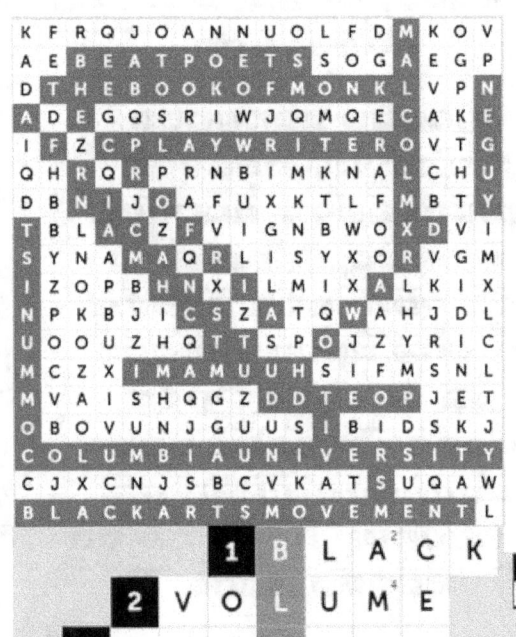

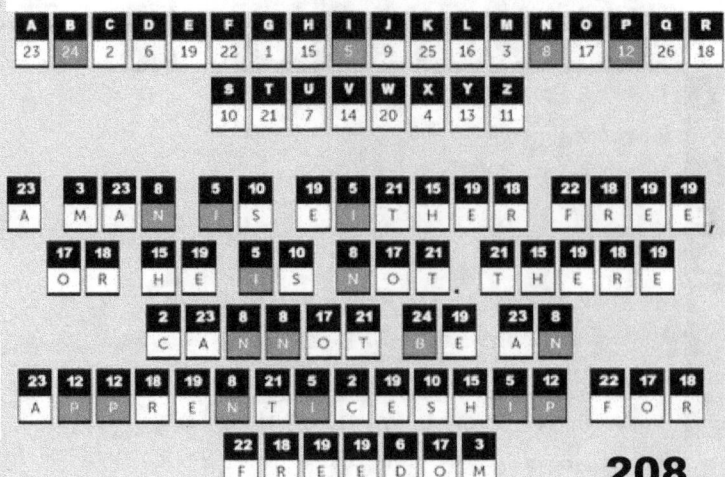

1. **What year did I become U.S. Poet Laureate?**
   A. 1987
   B. 1985
   C. 1986
2. **In what city did I grow up?**
   A. Topeka
   B. Chicago
   C. Tampa
3. **What award was I the first to win?**
   A. Poetry London Prize
   B. Pulitzer Prize
   C. Alice James Award

These are the steps to creating your own Ballad.

1) topic
2) Prose   rhyme
3) format
4) four
5) important
6) senses
7) naturally

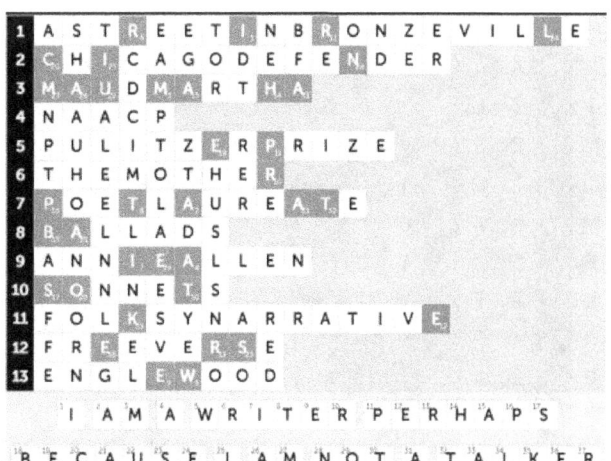

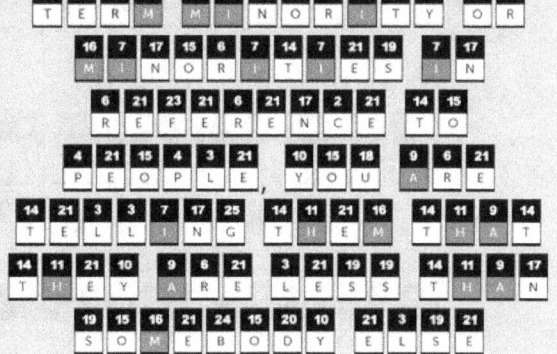

1. **What is not one of the issues I focused on?**
   A. civil rights
   B. fame
   C. urban life
2. **What was the name of the Magazine I worked for?**
   A. Time
   B. Life
   C. Ebony
3. **Which film didn't I direct?**
   A. Scarface
   B. Shaft
   C. The learning Tree

preview

overdo

rewrite

misjudge

nonstick

uncover

overboard

prevent

nonspecific

return

misplace

unlock

6 bonus word

Preview, uncover, prevent
return, misjudge, misplace

```
M W R S H A F T O X J E W E P U
M P B A T E C H N I Q U E C P Y
B N A Y C Q B Y U I C K X H N N
I A T L N I Z G M Y N R O A Q Y
M M D S U O S U L A X T M R B T
Q G E Q S Y B M Y V O E F V U R
M N N W M Q Y E M G C C U I Y E
R I O X L E O G R N C G W M M V
B G R F I V O A A L D T R M J O
J R W R F P P S L F U K T C A P
V E J A C H S K N I P S X R Q R
P M E F Y I W L K F T S E R B W
C E Y X A E N I Z G A M E F I L
J O G N D X U L W C A X N G E B
K S E O S D N B J C K Z W O G H
I R N O I T A N I M I R C S I D
```

1. B L A X P L O I T A T I O N
2. V O U G E
3. P A R I S
4. D U K E
5. B A L L E T
6. C O N S E R V A T I O N
7. L I F E
8. L E A R N I N G
9. P H O T O G R A P H Y

A	B	C	D	E	F	G	H	I	J	K	L	M	N	O	P	Q	R
10	22	12	15	5	6	9	21	1	13	17	8	7	16	26	11	19	20

S	T	U	V	W	X	Y	Z
3	14	2	24	4	25	18	23

14	21	5		3	2	22	13	5	12	14		7	10	14	14	5	20
T	H	E		S	U	B	J	E	C	T		M	A	T	T	E	R

1	3		3	26		7	2	12	21		7	26	20	5
I	S		S	O		M	U	C	H		M	O	R	E

1	7	11	26	20	14	10	16	14		14	21	10	16		14	21	5
I	M	P	O	R	T	A	N	T		T	H	A	N		T	H	E

11	21	26	14	26	9	20	11	21	5	20
P	H	O	T	O	G	R	P	H	E	R

1. What am I best know for?
  A. Children Books
  B. Art Work
  C. Quilts

2. How many children books have I published?
  A. 5
  B. 17
  C. 15

3. Which college did I attend?
  A. City College of New York
  B. Howard University
  C. New York University

Preposition answers
  1. for
  2. to
  3. on
  4. for
  5. from
  6. out
  7. to
  8. for
  9. for
  10. on
  11. with
  12. off

1. **What year did the Met feature Pool Parlor?**
   A. 1941
   B. 1942
   C. 1943
2. **What was my rank in the US Coast Guard?**
   A. Petty Officer First Class
   B. Petty Officer Third Class
   C. Petty Officer Second Class
3. **What event helped influence some of my work of art?**
   A. Franklin D Roosevelt getting elected to President
   B. The Depression
   C. World War I (WW I)

Answers may vary. Here are some suggested answers:

1) My dad works on a ship all day.

2) Our teacher, Professor Lawrence, assigned the class homework for the weekend.

3) We carefully looked through the paints to find the color green.

4) The little girl cried all day and night without stopping.

5) The Chief Petty Officer wears khaki pants and a tan shirt for his job.

6) Gwendolyn visited a friend on a rainy night.

7) The artist painted a portrait on the stage.

8) My sister found a script on the floor and looked really excited.

9) My wife, Gwendolyn, wears the fanciest dresses in the whole world.

10) My dad leaves the house and goes to work in Africa.

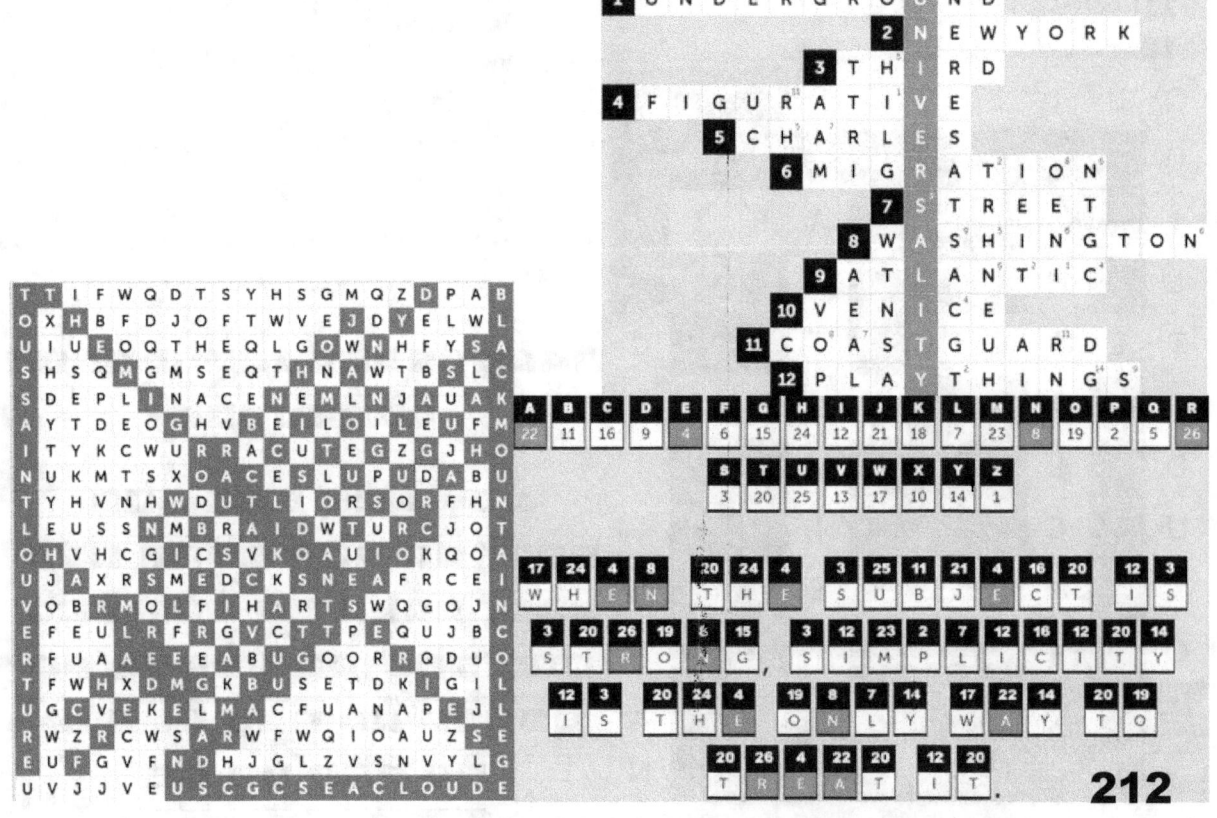

1. **What state was I born in?**
   A. Florida
   B. Georgia
   C. California

2. **What was the name of Magazine I was listed in?**
   A. Time
   B. The New Yorker
   C. Ebony

3. **Which work of art is not my own?**
   A. Pool Parlor
   B. Gone
   C. A Subtlety

Answers

Subject	1. The black paint.
Sentence	2. Octavia is tall.
Predicate	3. Walks to the museum.
Predicate	4. Lives in Fort Greene.
Subject	5. My art, Salvation.
Sentence	6. We saw the art show.
Subject	7. The sister of my uncle.
Predicate	8. Ate all of the candy.
Predicate	9. Wants to run a marathon.
Sentence	10. The nurse helps.
Subject	11. Octavia and Dana.
Sentence	12. Larry loves art.

Crossword grid:

```
                    ¹P
²C A L I ³F O R N I A
O        A      E
L        ⁴T     ⁵S C H A D
U        H     T
M     ⁵V E N I C E
B        R     G
I              I
A        ⁶I M P O S T E R
              U
⁷G E N I U S
```

1. R U T G E R S
2. F I L M A K E R
3. S I L H O U E T T I S T
4. C O N T E M P O R A R Y P A I N T E R
5. I N S T A L L A T I O N A R T I S T
6. A F T E R T H E D E L U G E
7. A S U B T L E T Y
8. F O N A M E R I C A N U S
9. V I E N N A S T A T E O P E R A
10. U N I V E R S I T Y O F M I C H I G A N

¹V ²I ³S U A L A ⁷R ⁸T ⁹S¹⁰

A	B	C	D	E	F	G	H	I	J	K	L	M	N	O	P	Q	R
6	4	19	17	10	2	24	25	3	14	15	11	9	13	16	5	21	7

S	T	U	V	W	X	Y	Z
23	22	12	20	26	1	18	8

3	25	6	20	10		13	16		3	13	22	10	7	10	23	22
I	H	A	V	E		N	O		I	N	T	E	R	E	S	T

3	13		9	6	15	3	13	24		6		26	16	7	15
I	N		M	A	K	I	N	G		A		W	O	R	K

22	25	6	22		17	16	10	23		13	16	22
T	H	A	T		D	O	E	S		N	O	T

10	11	3	19	3	22		6		2	10	10	11	3	13	24
E	L	I	C	I	T		A		F	E	E	L	I	N	G
```
```

1. **In WW I who did I serve with?**
   A. Infantry
   B. Red Cross
   C. Cooks
2. **I became a member of the National Academy of Design in?**
   A. 1920
   B. 1927
   C. 1930
3. **What city was my Academy in?**
   A. Pittsburgh
   B. Scranton
   C. Philadelphia

Word search grid containing:
REALIST PAINTER, RED CROSS

Crossword:
1. PENNSYLVANIA
2. INTERNATIONAL
3. CELEBRITY
4. FOCUSING
5. MOTHER
6. GENRE

Letter-number key:
A	B	C	D	E	F	G	H	I	J	K	L	M	N	O	P	Q	R
20	11	22	9	19	13	18	23	12	26	5	17	15	7	16	3	8	25

S	T	U	V	W	X	Y	Z
6	21	1	10	24	4	14	2

I WILL PREACH WITH MY BRUSH.

1. **What college didn't I go to?**
   A. Oberlin College
   B. Michigan University
   C. New York Central College
2. **What year did I participate in Centennial Exposition?**
   A. 1920
   B. 1876
   C. 1870
3. **What is one of my inspiration?**
   A. WW I heroes
   B. WW II heroes
   C. Abolitionists

Match each term with its definition.

1) H
2) A
3) I
4) B
5) G
6) D
7) F
8) E

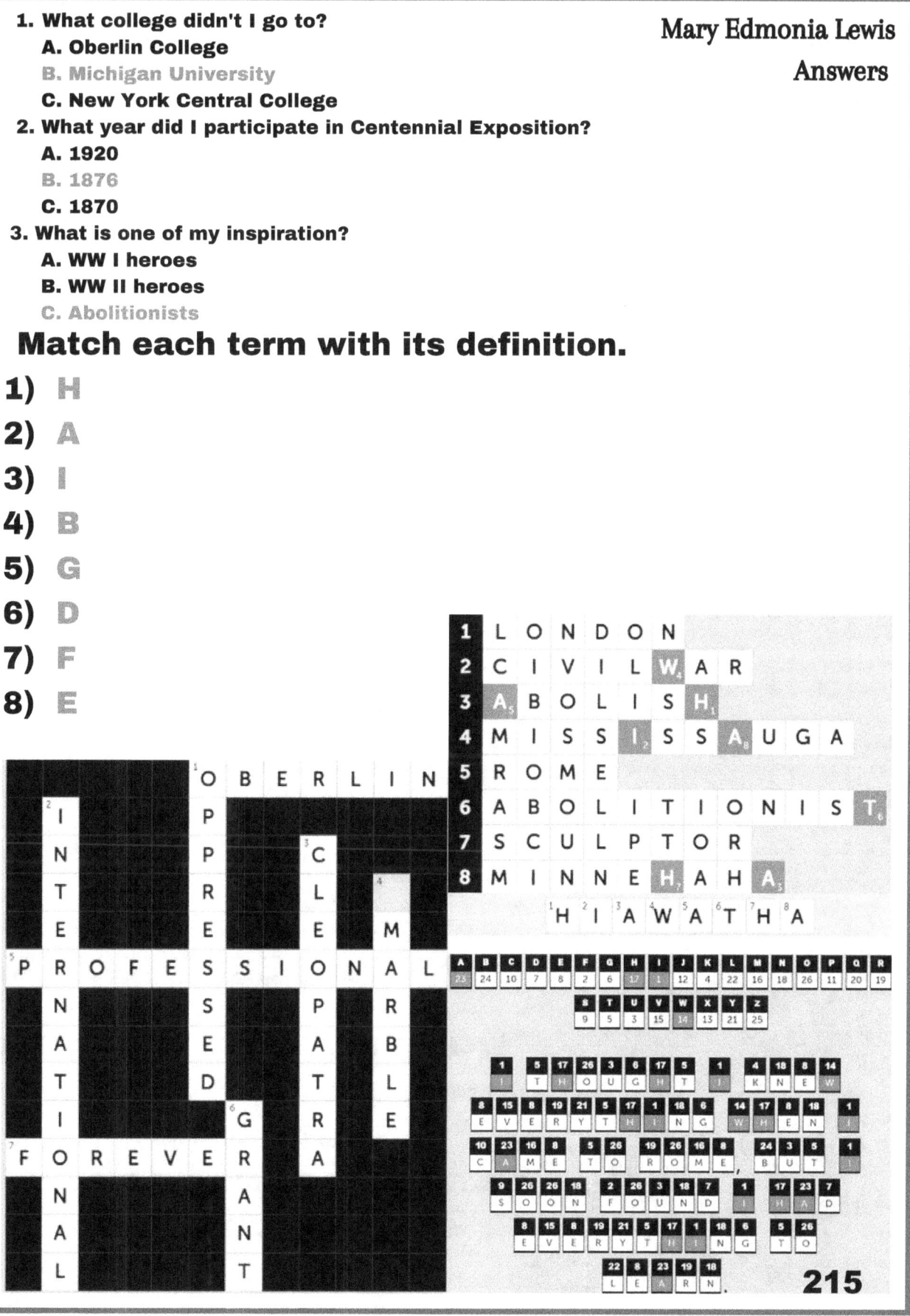

1. **What am I know for?**
   A. Movies
   B. Jazz Poetry
   C. Children Books
2. **What is the name of my fraternity?**
   A. Alpha Phi Alpha
   B. Omega Psi Phi
   C. Kappa Alpha Psi
3. **What city was I born in?**
   A. Chicago
   B. Joplin
   C. Philadelphia

Continents

Spain	Europe
Soviet Union	Asia/ Europe
China	Asia
Washington D.C.	North America
Japan	Asia
Haiti	North America
Korea	Asia
Madrid	Europe
New York	North America
Turkmenistan	Asia

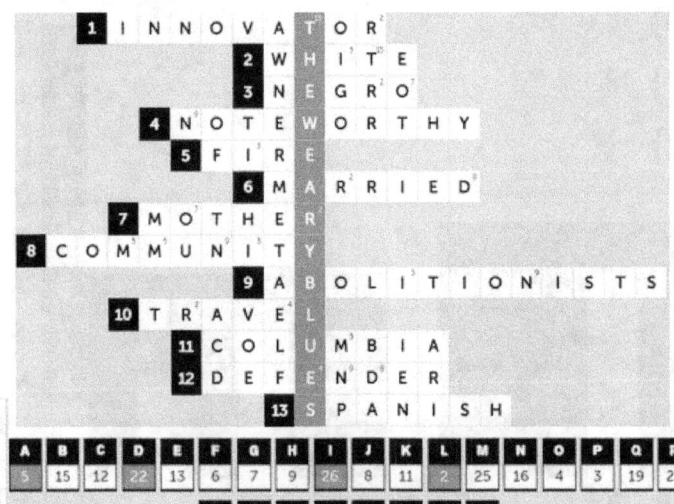

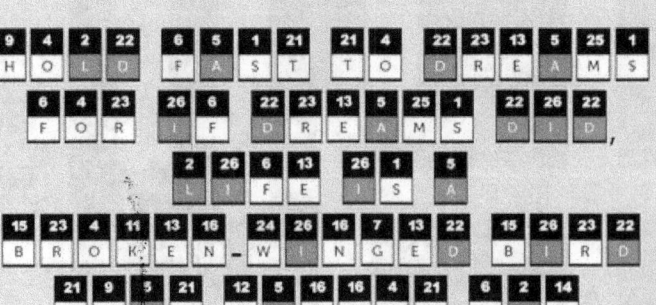

1. **What was my dream job as a teen?**
   A. Cook
   B. Streetcar Conductor
   C. Poet
2. **What poem did I win a Grammy for?**
   A. Still I Rise
   B. On The Pulse of Morning
   C. The Heart of a Woman
3. **What city did I attend school?**
   A. Pittsburgh
   B. San Francisco
   C. New York

My beautiful black queens

1) Clever, innovative and beautiful

2) The hype

3) Taint means a trace of a bad or undesirable quality or substance.

4) Your black, your ugly, you're a woman

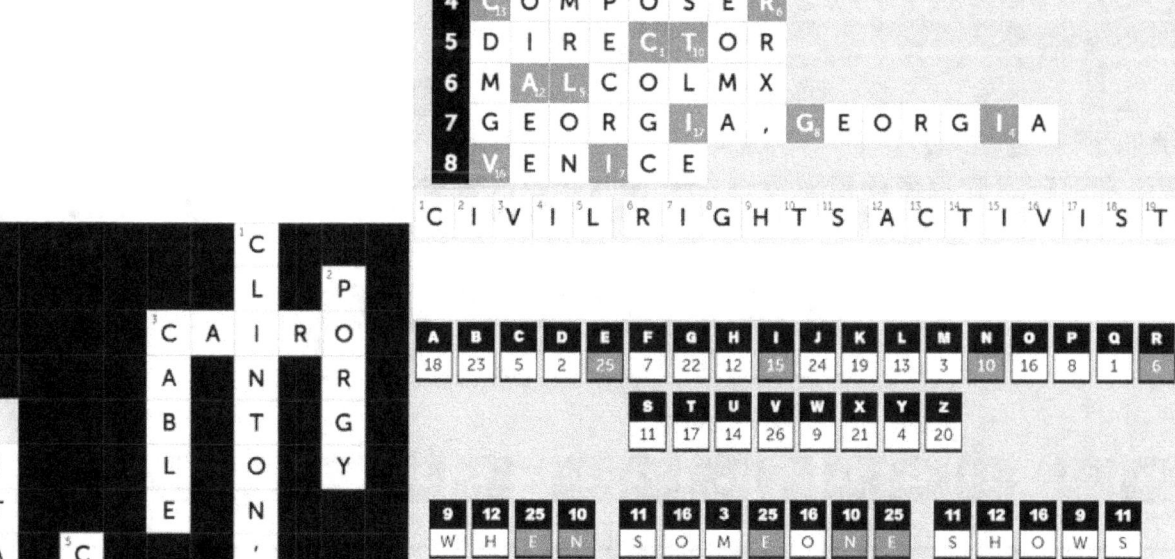

1. **What year did I enlist in the Army?**
   A. 1950
   B. 1947
   C. 1948
2. **What did I go to prison for?**
   A. selling drugs
   B. assault
   C. armed robbery
3. **What poet didn't visit me in prison?**
   A. Langston Hughes
   B. Sonia Sanchez
   C. Gwendolyn Brooks

Circle the word that correctly completes each sentence.

1) earning
2) members
3) serving
4) published
5) learned
6) wounded

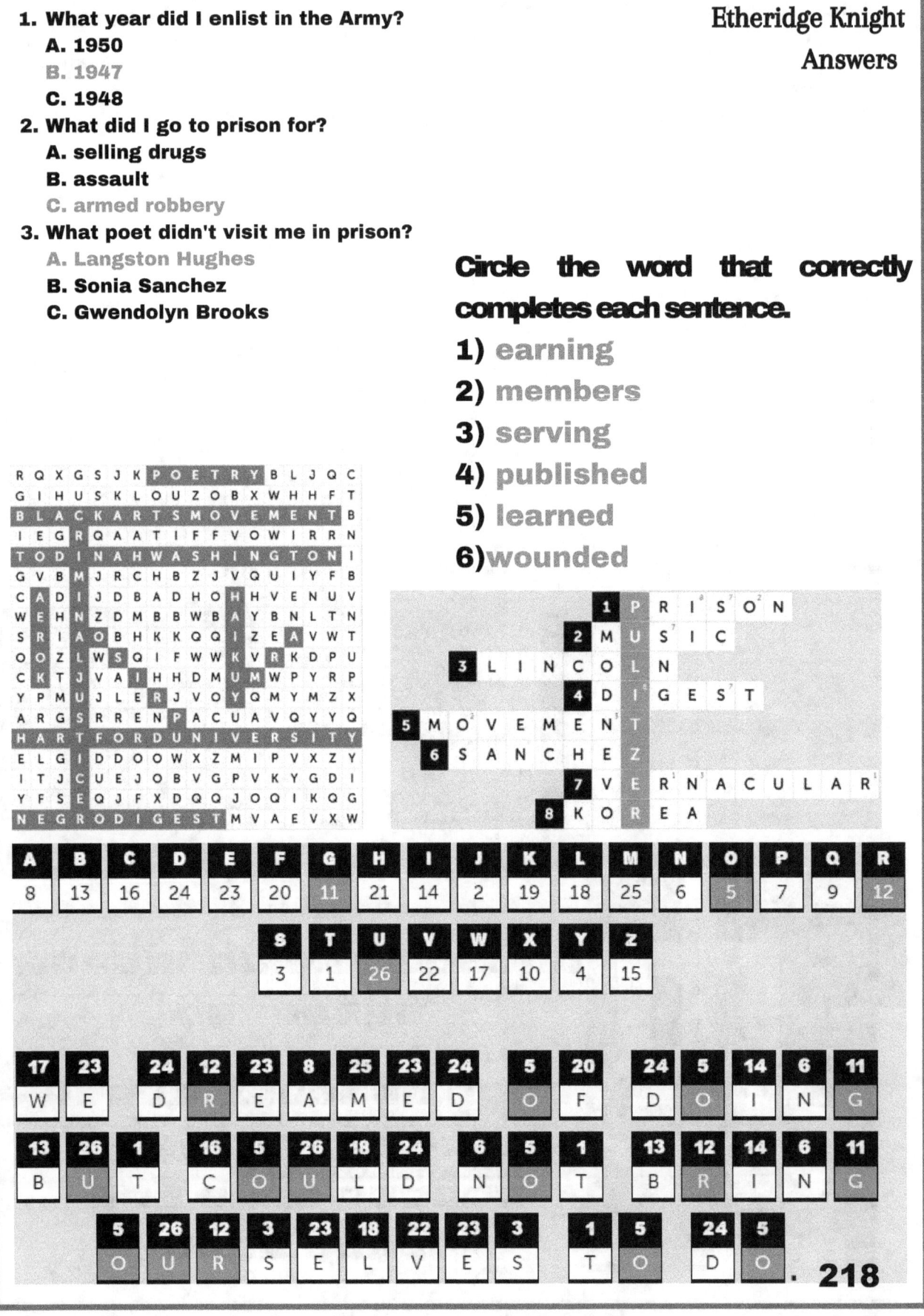

1. **What is my highest level of education?**
   A. **Bachelors Degree**
   B. Ph.D.
   C. **Masters Degree**
2. **What University did I teach at?**
   A. **University of Iowa**
   B. Jackson State University
   C. **Northwestern University**
3. **What year did I get inducted into The Chicago Literary HOF?**
   A. **1998**
   B. **2000**
   C. 2014

Capitalize sentences

1) My favorite book is "Jubilee".
2) For Christmas, we listen to "Jingle Bells" and dress like Elves.
3) On Friday, my mom is taking me shopping in Illinois for new Nike shoes.
4) My grandma visits Orlando in June.
5) We read "For My People" by Margaret Walker last August.
6) On Tuesday, President Kennedy will be honored in Washington, D. C.
7) I learned about President Obama in a book called "A Promised Land".
8) For Memorial Day, we visit my grandpa in Mississippi.

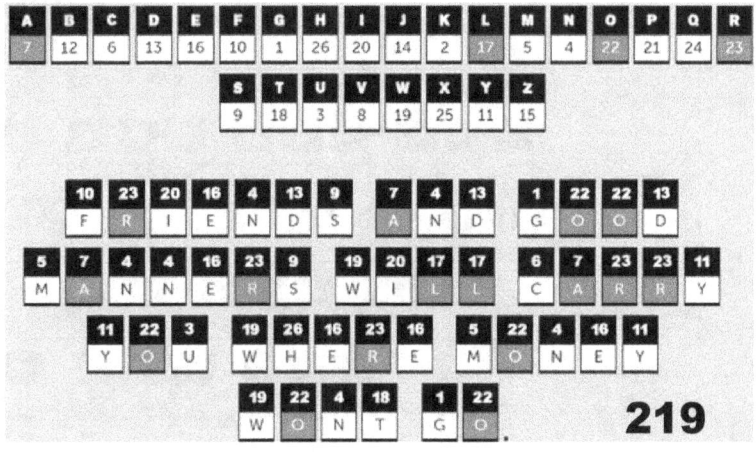

219

1. **What was my pseudonym name?**
   A. Milo
   B. SAMO
   C. Skana
2. **What was the video I appeared in?**
   A. Fight the power
   B. Rapture
   C. Rock the bells
3. **What museum hosted my exhibition?**
   A. Metropolitan Museum of Art
   B. Brooklyn Museum
   C. The Frick

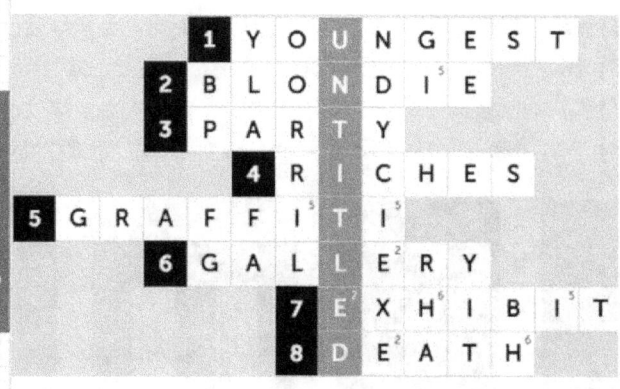

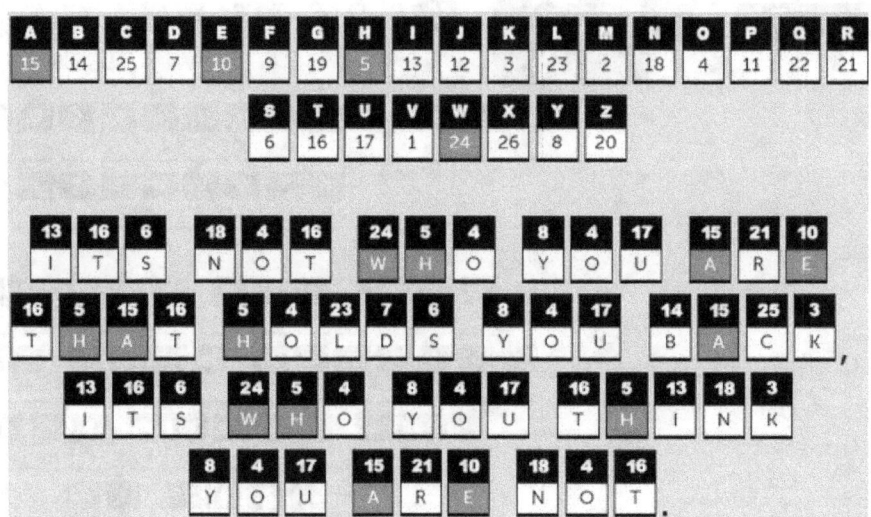

1. **Which book is one of mine?**
   A. Lead From the Outside
   B. I Am Not Your Negro
   C. Jim Crow: The Sequel

2. **What year did I publish my first book?**
   A. 1970
   B. 1969
   C. 1968

3. **What did I want everyone to respect?**
   A. Each other
   B. Them selves
   C. Black English

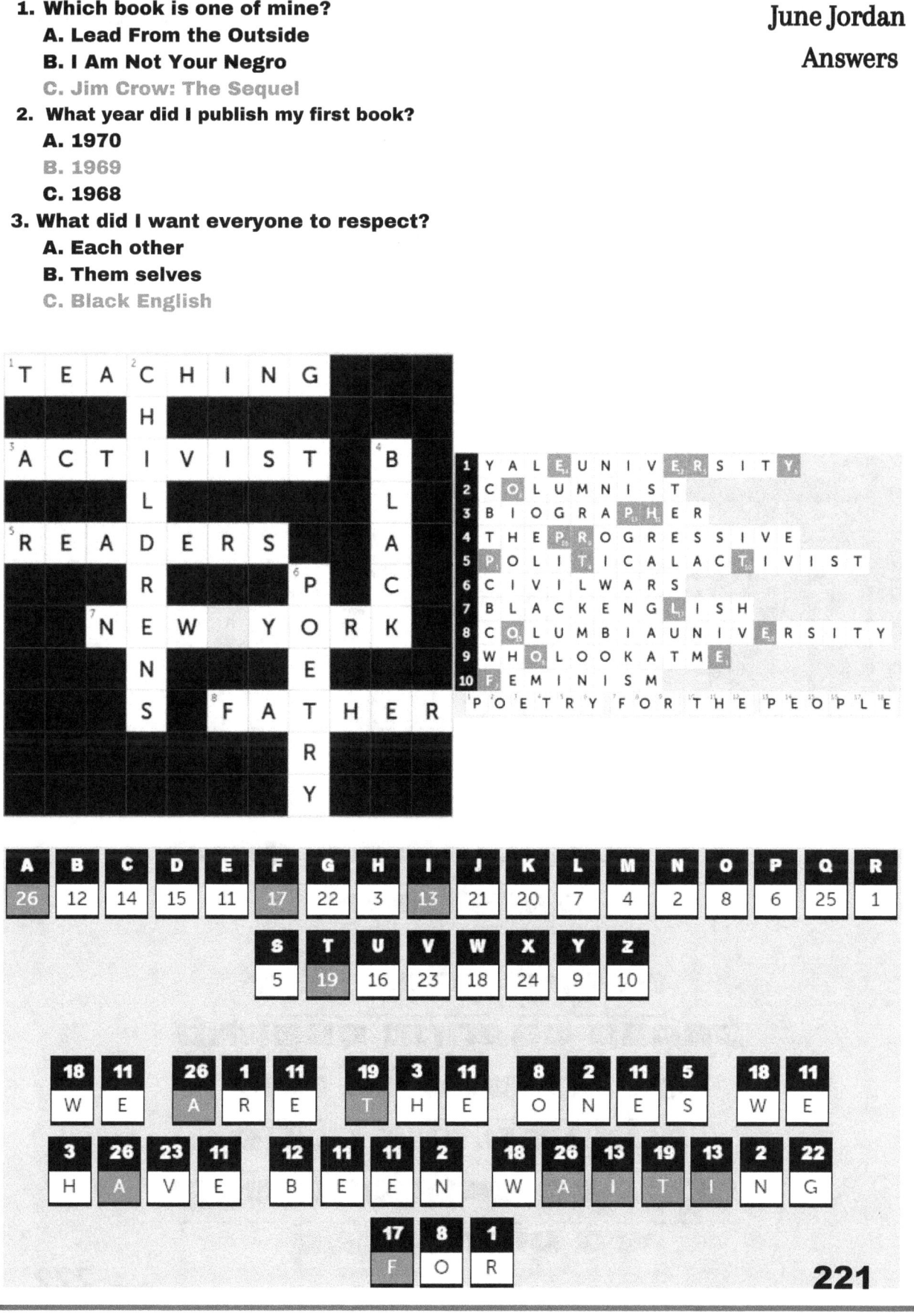

1. **What college did I go to?**
   A. Jackson State University
   B. Atlanta University
   C. Ohio State University
2. **What is Life Every Voice and sing know as?**
   A. The love Anthem
   B. The National Anthem
   C. The Negro National Anthem
3. **How old was I when I enrolled in college?**
   A. 18
   B. 16
   C. 20

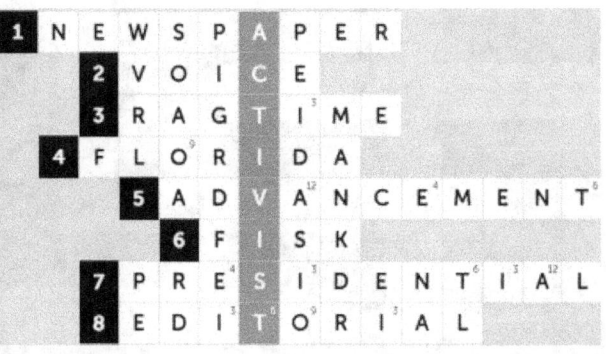

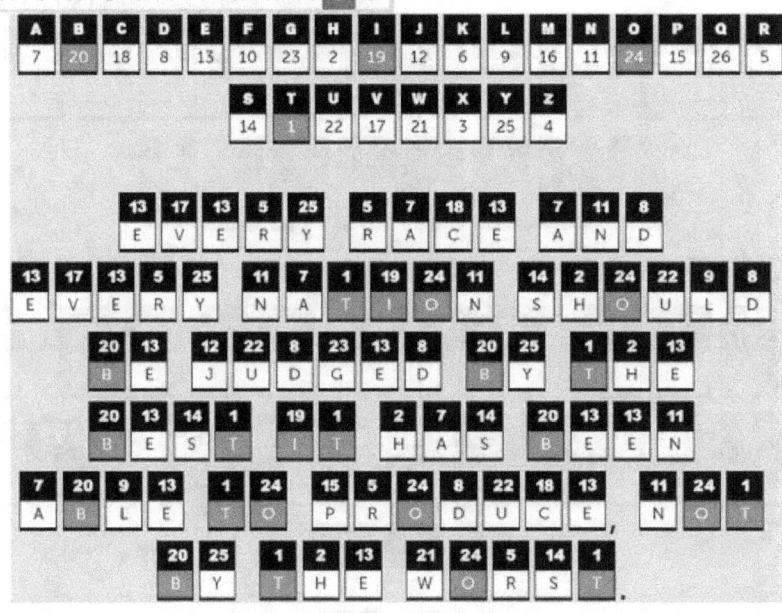

1. How did I get my first name?
   A. From my parents
   B. From my slave owner
   C. From the ship
2. What year did I publish my first book?
   A. 1770
   B. 1774
   C. 1773
3. I was the first person of African descent to what?
   A. Come to America
   B. Have my work published
   C. Get my freedom

Adjective or Adverbs

1.) Adverb
2.) Adjective
3.) Adjective
4.) Adjective
5.) Adverb
6.) Adverb
7.) Adjective
8.) Adverb

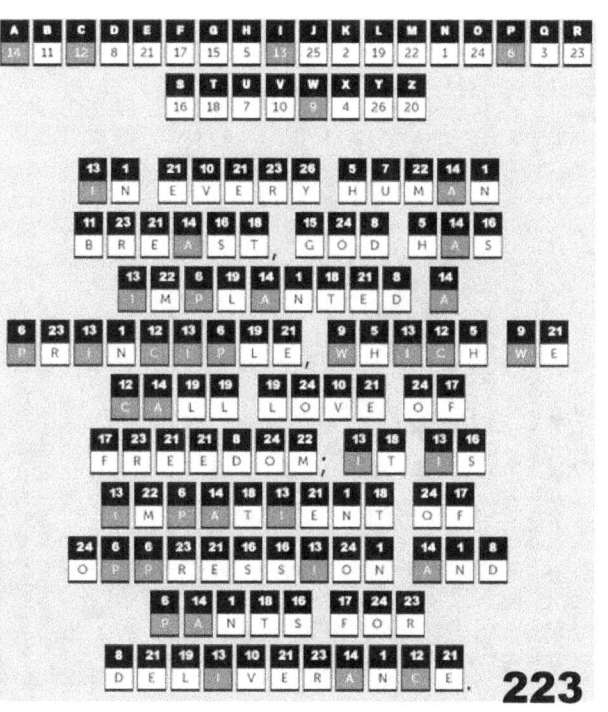

1. **What year did I publish my first book?**
   A. 1912
   B. 1909
   C. 1912
2. **What University didn't I attend?**
   A. Tuskegee University
   B. Kansas State University
   C. Howard University
3. **What is not one of my books?**
   A. A Long Way from Home
   B. Invisible Man
   C. Home to Harlem

Past	Present	Future
Walked	pull	will teach
Bought	begin	will greet
Was eating	catch	will be sliding
Ate	is playing	will drink
Was touching	is jogging	will drive

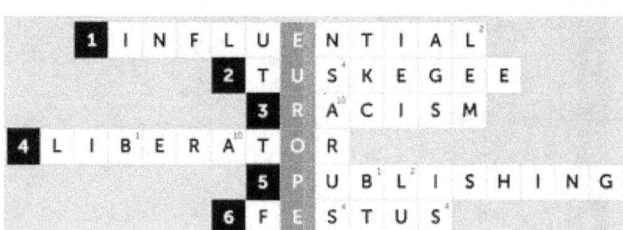

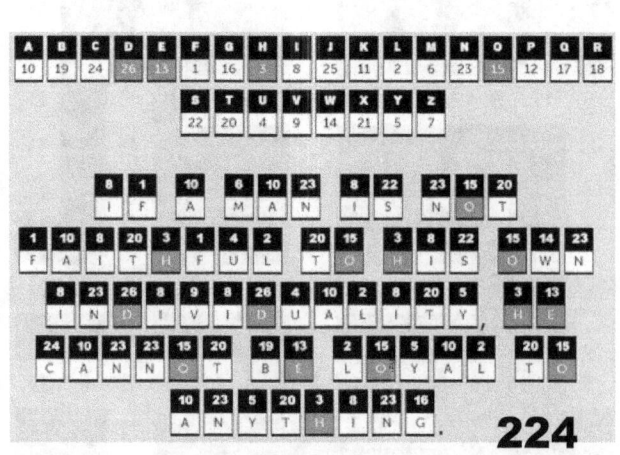

224

1. **What University did I graduate from?**
   A. **Jackson State**
   B. **Spellman**
   C. Fisk
2. **What inspired some of my work?**
   A. **College**
   B. Civil Rights Movement
   C. **Growing Up**
3. **What city was I born in?**
   A. Knoxville
   B. **Scranton**
   C. **Philadelphia**

Combine the Sentences

1) Brutus, Trixie and Mary are my pets.
2) The uncle, the kids, and the parents went to dinner.
3) She was sad because she lost her purse, failed her driving test, and forgot her mom's dinner.
4) We bought a candy, some food, and some drinks.
5) Amy, Matt, and Nikki are my cousins.
6) This pot is hot, big, and dirty.
7) My dad eats ham, eggs, and grits.
8) This poet writes, lectures, and teaches.

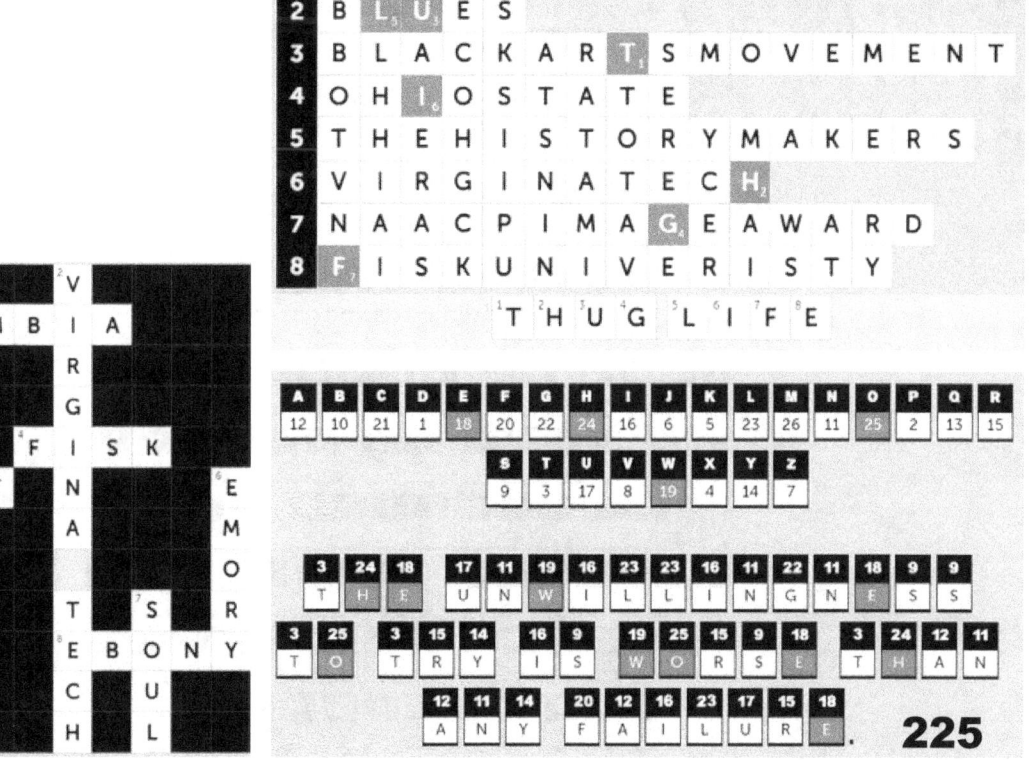

1. **Who was my classmate in High School?**
   A. **Frederick Douglass**
   B. Orville Wright
   C. **James Johnson**
2. **What made my work unique?**
   A. **Metaphors**
   B. Dialectic
   C. **My use of Haiku**
3. **What city was my High Shool in?**
   A. **Columbus**
   B. **Youngstown**
   C. Dayton

Pronouns

1) possessive
2) indefinite
3) relative
4) relative
5) possessive
6) possessive
7) indefinite
8) indefinite

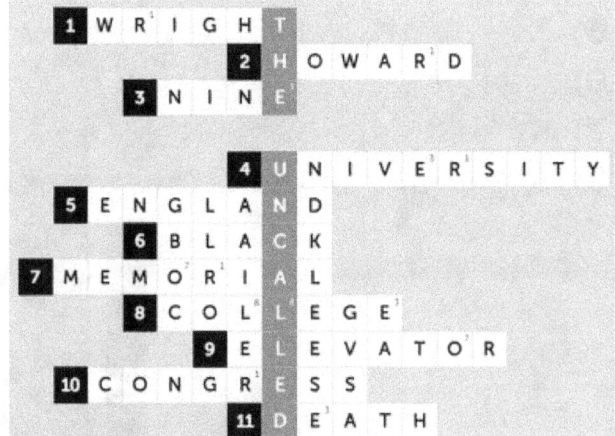

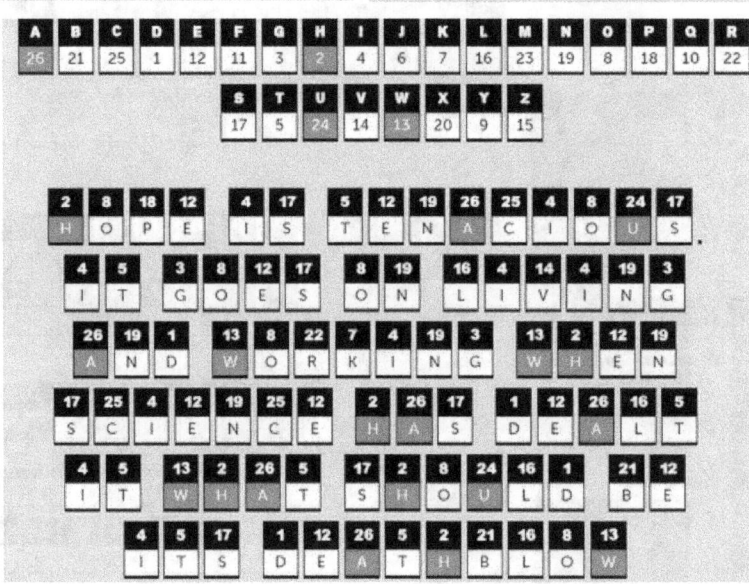

1. **What did I first aspire to be?**
   A. Photographer
   B. Pianist
   C. Violinist
2. **What years did I become know as the eyes of Harlem?**
   A. 1920s
   B. 1910s
   C. 1930s
3. **What parade did I capture pictures for?**
   A. Macy Day
   B. Universal Negro Improvement Association
   C. Memorial Day

Circle the verbs in the sentences.

1) ordered
2) scared   screamed
3) reached
4) picked   threw
5) measure   pour
6) am   sing
7) barked
8) served
9) watched
10) were   stood

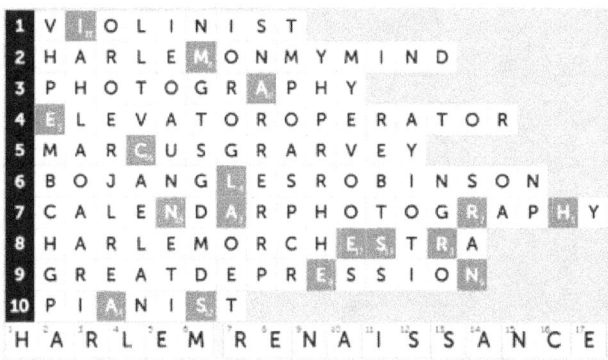

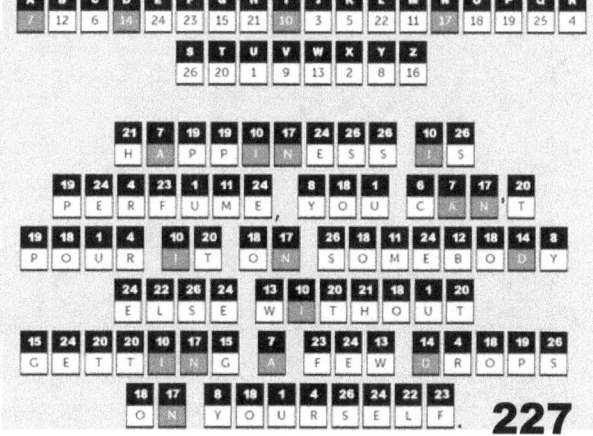

227

This book is dedicated to my grandkids
Anais Isabella Pablo-Antonio
Deyshawn Frank Chambers
Alicia Marie Jackson
Ayianna Marie Chambers
Zion Jamaris Jackson
Jayvon Jerome Jackson
Camilla Claire Hale
Truen Christopher Jackson

ABOUT THE AUTHOR

Matthew D. Hale is a retired United States Marine, disabled veteran, computer engineer, educator, and author of the **Black Historical Figures Activity Workbook** series. Matthew created his books with one mission in mind: to teach history that was made, but too often not taught, celebrated, or remembered. Through his work, he shines a light on Black historical figures whose courage, brilliance, leadership, creativity, and contributions helped shape the world. As an author, Matthew believes learning should be more than reading words on a page. His workbooks are designed to make history interactive, engaging, and memorable. Each book combines biographies, reading activities, questions, puzzles, grammar exercises, crossword puzzles, writing prompts, and quizzes to help children not only learn about important Black historical figures, but also think deeply about their impact. Matthew's books are used by parents, teachers, churches, daycares, schools, and community programs to help students build knowledge, confidence, and cultural pride. His goal is to create educational resources that children want to use, parents value, and educators can trust. With a Master's Degree in Computer Engineering and a lifelong commitment to service, Matthew brings both structure and creativity to his educational work. His background as a Marine taught him discipline, perseverance, and leadership, while his passion for education drives him to create tools that help young people see greatness in history and possibility in themselves. Through his books and his educational platform, **We Gonna Learn Today**, Matthew continues to build resources that make Black History, financial literacy, civics, and learning more accessible to students and families everywhere.

At the heart of Matthew D. Hale's work is a simple belief:

When children learn the truth about history, they gain pride, purpose, and power.

"In order to grow we must visit uncomfortable places"

10 ACTIVITY WORKBOOK SERIES

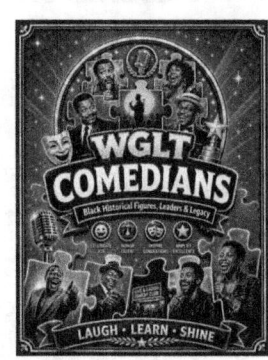

GET YOUR COPY TOAY

DON'T FORGET TO TELL A FRIEND